Loyal

to

Love

A NOVEL BY

Tori D.

ISBN: 978-0-692-21302-5

Cover: Davida Baldwin
www.oddballdsgn.com

Editors: Carla Dean
www.ucanmarkmyword.com

Twenty-First Street Urban Editing
www.21streeturbanediting.com

Typesetting: Twenty-First Street Urban Editing
www.21StreetUrbanEditing.com

www.loyaltolove.com

Acknowledgements

After eight long years of writing, revising, doubt, and rewriting, I found the strength, courage, and God's grace to deliver my baby!

First and foremost, I must give glory to God for providing me with the gift and words to make this book possible for you to read. This book would not have been possible without God's love, grace, and mercy upon my life.

My first love, and the leading man, boy-o-boy, what a journey! I thank you for being there for me and loving me through it all. We have a bond for life and I love you for molding me and teaching me all that you have. Thank you!

Karhma, my sissy, my encouragement, my strength, my second breath, thank you! Thank you for always listening to my dreams, stories, and ideas. You play a huge part in my everyday existence and I couldn't ask for anything more.

Mom and Dad, thank you both; without the two of you there would be no me. Mom, thank you for always being my backbone. I love you unconditionally!

Kelli, my childhood cherry on the top, my love for you will never fade no matter where life takes us. Thank you for being there for me, listening to my cries, and always having my back.

Ellena and my "second family," I love you all. Thank you for being there for me and accepting me into your family.

I thank all of my family and friends for being patient and riding it out with me until my book was developed. I appreciate your unconditional love and support and I hope you enjoy reading *Desiree's journey*.

Be Blessed,
Tori D.

Chapter One

I've always imaged that the ultimate fairy tale relationship for a girl growing up in the hood was to find the sexiest hustler with the most money who would vow to be with you and *only you* until death do you part. Girls make sure they keep their innocence, tight shapes, and youth intact just in case they happen to come up on the man of their dreams. It's sort of like an auction. We look our finest to get selected by the best man on the grind, and pray that we don't end up with an abusive or controlling man in the process.

Unfortunately, we never seem to look past the glitter and gold to learn the true story behind a hustler's life. Females expect to sit back and reap the benefits of being *that girl*. They fight hard, and at times, with each other for that title, but there's always a dark side of the relationship the girlfriend never wants outsiders to know about. This time, I'm telling mine.

From my early teens, I made up my mind that I wouldn't be the type of girl who would be left struggling to raise kids alone or be controlled by an abusive man like my mother had done for many of my childhood years. We had to move from the comforts of our suburban family home to a rundown apartment in the hood, which turned me into the beast I became. I knew I had the brains and the banging body to get any man I wanted, and I wasn't going to settle for less.

I learned a lot growing up in the hood. I was constantly reminded by my mother that you had to take advantage of every situation when it came to men. If girls aren't smart enough to take advantage of them, they will definitely be taken advantage of. That is, totally naïve females who lack street smarts and common sense. I wasn't about to settle for any man that had money, but "The Man" with an abundance of cash, that was willing and able to spoil me generously.

Every now and then, I would play around with nickel and dime hustlers who claimed to have a bank roll. But their little rolls only took them so far with me. They paid for clothes, groceries, my hair, and nails. But nothing major, because I knew they would expect something in return, and I wasn't giving it up.

I looked up to the older chicks who held it down for their men. I admired how they were highly compensated for their dedication, being that down-ass chick. I wanted to be just like them with the fly rides, diamonds, and purses from all the major designers. I didn't want to be just a material girl that looked good on the outside and had nothing going on inside my brain. I also planned to go to school, get a degree, and hold my man down, all while remaining fly. I wanted the younger females look up to me and my relationship for all the positive aspects I represented.

I didn't want to be the girl who sat around and sucked up all my man's money, forcing him to have to stay out extra hours at night to make up what I spent. Whoever I ended up with, together, we were going to be unstoppable and build a memorable empire that would go down in history. That is, if all went as I planned.

If it was up to me, I would be able to live my fairy tale life, in my fairy tale dream, with my fairy tale man. But like all dreams, you wake up and have to deal with the harsh facts of reality. You either have to look past all the superficial things and skillfully play the hand you've been dealt, or fold. I wasn't the quitting type, so I put my poker face on and let the games begin.

Chapter Two

Thanksgiving was supposed to be a day where you celebrated what you were most thankful for, and I was grateful to spend the holiday with the man of my dreams and his wonderful family. I hurt sometimes that I didn't have my own family around to share laughs and childhood memories with. Fortunately, I was accepted with open arms into my new family whom I loved and cherished dearly.

My mom moved out of the hood, a couple years back, into a small apartment in Indiana and left me to live with my boyfriend, Cee, about three years ago, when she saw that he could take care of me better than she could. Sometimes, I felt like an orphan, adopted by a wonderful family who took me in and treated me like I belonged. I was most thankful to have an extended family to call my own and a wonderful man who loved and adored me.

"Good morning, Marie. Happy Thanksgiving," I said sweetly as I answered my phone while watching a Thanksgiving re-run of *Girlfriends*.

"Happy Thanksgiving to you, Desiree. Has Cee come home yet?" Cee's mother asked.

"No, I haven't talked to him since this morning. Why? What's up?"

"Are you sitting down? I have something to tell you," said Marie seriously.

I started to laugh. "No, I'm not sitting. I'm actually lying down in my bed. What's wrong?"

"Well," Marie sighed then continued. "I shouldn't be telling you this, but this has gone on for too long. You know I love you like my daughter, and this is hard for me to just come out and say... I take it Cee hasn't told you?"

I sensed the hesitation in Marie's voice, telling me that this was a serious issue. She was trying to break the news to me as sweetly as possible, because she knew I could be a firecracker at times. Marie tried to refrain from interfering between relationship issues with Cee and I, but would hint around from time to time if he was getting out of line. She never directly told on her son when she hinted around about what he was doing, but instead let me use my own common sense to figure out what was going on, and I couldn't blame her.

She was ecstatic when her son told her that he'd finally found someone special who was good to him and wasn't trying to use him for his money. Marie and I clicked immediately and got along a little too well. She treated me like a daughter and didn't hold back when it came to keeping it real and putting me in my place when my mouth got out of line. She appreciated how I took charge and made Cee come home every night with no ifs, ands, or buts about it. She was relieved and slept peacefully, knowing that she no longer had to worry herself sick about her son's safety while he stayed out all night in the streets.

I loved and respected Marie to the fullest. So, her having to tell me something had me all ears.

"Told me what, Marie?"

"About Darius."

"Who is Darius?" I said slowly, getting upset that Marie wasn't getting to the point. Beatin' around bushes wasn't my specialty.

"Desiree, Cee has a little boy and his birthday is today. I told Cee to tell you before he left for the birthday party. It hasn't been fair that our family has known about and met Darius while you are still in the dark. I'm sorry, Desi."

"Marie, is this some sort of a joke?" I began to chuckle.

I must have been on *Punk'd* or *Candid Camera*, because there was no way in hell my man's mother was on the other end of my phone seriously telling me that he had an illegitimate child and it was the kid's birthday!

"No, Desiree, I'm sorry it isn't. I felt you deserved to know, and Cee was taking too long to speak up," said Marie softly.

"So I take it you knew all this time and waited until today to decide to tell me!" I replied, getting loud while sitting on the edge of my bed.

Marie remained silent.

"Who else knows about this kid?" I asked, feeling a sense of embarrassment.

"Just our family that I know of. I'm so sorry, Desiree. It wasn't our place to tell you; it was Cee's." Marie paused so I could gather my thoughts then continued. "I'm going to let you go now so you can calm down and discuss this with Cee when he comes home. Happy Thanksgiving, baby," Marie concluded, and hung up.

Blankly, I stared at my phone. I was hurt, confused, and mad all at the same time. Various emotions flooded my brain, disabling my thought process.

"What the fuck!" I screamed aloud to no one.

What is going on here? This is Thanksgiving for goodness sake. What type of shit is this to be thankful for?

I couldn't understand what was actually going on or begin to comprehend the revelation of this news. I needed answers. I needed to know who this baby was and who in the hell was this female that Cee had to have slept with to conceive this child. Why hadn't he told me that he could possibly be someone's father, especially after everything we had been through? We agreed to always be upfront and honest, no matter how hurtful the news. I felt my blood begin to boil inside my body as I angrily punched the numbers to Cee's cell.

"Hey, gorgeous, you ready to go over to Mom's and chow down?" Cee chimed into the phone, obviously oblivious.

"Where the fuck are you, Cee?" I asked, fuming inside, not in the mood for petty chit-chat.

"Damn, what's wrong with you, Desi? I'm in the car on the way. Why?

"Get the fuck home now, and I mean now!" I screamed into the phone. "And don't make any miscellaneous stops either!"

I disconnected the call and immediately started crying hysterically on my bed, kicking and screaming like a mad woman.

Cee and I had been through some shit in the past, like him having to bail me out of jail for fighting jealous hoes and us constantly arguing because chicks wouldn't stop calling and playing on his phone, but nothing like this. Of course, I would be the one to initiate the arguments because I had to put everybody in check to let them know I wasn't one to be fucked with.

Overall, even through the stressful madness, we managed to stick together. He made all the outside problems vanish and kept me happy. The drama with chicks in the past was temporary, but this shit was live and in the flesh. What could I possibly say or do this time to make a situation like this go away? I would be less of a woman to say forget about that child or not allow Cee to be in the child's life. This was too much to handle, the thoughts in my head whirled like a tornado, causing a migraine to emerge.

I didn't know what to do, what to think, or how to react. But my first thought was, *this bastard has to go.*

There was no way I would be able to contain myself in the same house around him. Whenever I was provoked and became amped up in a rage, I didn't stop or shut up until I heard whatever I wanted to hear or had successfully proven my point. I wasn't mentally stable at this point, so I had to make the best move for me.

I slammed the phone on the charger, grabbed some trash bags from the kitchen, and ran back upstairs. Ignoring the constantly ringing phone as Cee continuously called back to back, I stormed into the second bedroom where Cee's clothes were and started ripping clothes from hangers like Bernadine in *Waiting to Exhale.* Lord, did I feel her pain.

Every expensive brand of clothes you could think of was shoved into trash bags like cheap rags. I filled them and then began tossing out his shoes. Every item he had in here had to get the hell out of my house. I didn't give a fuck; everything had to go.

My mind was racing, thinking all kinds of crazy thoughts. At one point, I felt as if my body was one place and my mind was somewhere else. I felt defeated, because once again, I'd lost the battle of keeping my man to myself. I knew the news would leak out and swarm the streets, putting my name to shame.

Still in a rage, my eyes began to swell as I cried harder. I hated having to throw him out because it was really his house, and I couldn't afford to pay for anything without him. I knew in my heart I didn't want him to go, but I couldn't understand how he could keep something this serious from me. We were at the stage in our relationship where I felt like no one could come between us. I had nothing but unconditional love and trust for him until this point.

I began questioning myself. *How could I believe this information is even true? Could Marie be mistaken? Had Cee even taken a blood test? Should I trust him if he says it's not true?*

I refused to let myself be in denial or naïve. Ignoring all the miscellaneous thoughts and questions in my mind, I threw my hands up and said fuck it. The truth was he had been taking care of a damn child and had the audacity to parade him around his family. Fucking Bastard!

About twenty minutes later, while I was in the process of tossing the overstuffed trash bags down the steps, Cee stormed in and slammed the front door behind him, screaming my name.

"Desiree! Desiree! What the fuck are you doing?" Cee screamed up the steps to me. He was visibly upset, but kept his distance because he didn't know what was going on in my head.

"No, the question is, where the fuck you been and what have you been doing? Huh?" I asked, fuming, shouting from the top of the stairs. I hiked back into the room and grabbed another stuffed bag.

Cee ran up the stairs. "I was out with Will. What's all this about?" He asked, waving his hands around at the mess I had made in our bedroom.

"Oh really? Well, how was your baby's birthday party, Cee, huh? What you get him?" I asked with my hands on my hips, standing face-to-face so I could see his reaction before he tried to come up with a lie.

He instantly dropped his head, as he always did when he was lying. I knew he was with Will earlier, but I also knew he was good for telling partial lies. He always managed to tell me half the truth about where he was and what he was doing, leaving out whatever he didn't want me to know.

"Yeah, I knew it. Can't talk now? Embarrassed are ya? Well, you should be! Now you can go play family with your son. He needs you, baby. I don't," I lied, then grabbed another bag and tried walking pass Cee as he stood there looking stupid.

Roughly, he grabbed me from behind and snatched the large bag from my hands. He stood silent and held me tight as I fought, trying to wrestle my way out of his strong grip. The last place I wanted to be was in his arms, but the tighter he held me, the less I tried to break free of him. Worn out and defeated, I calmed down. The hard role I was trying to play went straight out the window. Tears burned my eyes as they streamed down my face. Internally, I fought with myself because I wanted him to let me go, but something else inside wanted to stay in his arms forever.

"Why, Cee? Why?" I cried loudly.

He leaned his head on my shoulder and whispered softly in my ear, "I'm sorry, Desi."

"You should be, dummy!" I said, growing with anger. I tried hysterically to fight my way out of his grip, but I was too weak. "Let go of me, Cee. I obviously don't mean shit to you. We been together for five years and I still can't trust you. I don't deserve this. I have been nothing but good to you. You don't love me. Let me go!" I screamed.

"I do love you, Desi. You know I do. I don't even know if that kid is mine," he said as he turned me around to face him.

"But you've been taking care of that child. You must have some feelings toward him since you had the nerve to take him around your family. What type of shit is that? When were you going tell me? When the damn kid turned eighteen?"

"Today," he said softly, loosening his grip from around my body. He kept his head bowed to prevent making eye contact. He kept trying to hug me, but I wouldn't stay still.

"Well, thank you for enlightening me, Daddy. And you know what? Fuck you, fuck your kid, and fuck your fake-ass family. I'm out. And, oh yeah...Happy Thanksgiving."

I shook myself from Cee's grip, ran down the steps, grabbed my purse and car keys, and ran out the house without ever looking back.

I'm not sure what hurt me more, the fact he actually admitted to the situation or how blind I was the entire time. He betrayed my trust and that hurt me to my core. I never sexually cheated on Cee, even when all of the tramps claimed they were messing around with him, bragging about what he had done for them.

He bought me all sorts of gifts to make up for my pain and assured me those females were all telling lies. I knew he was only trying to top the gifts the hoes said he bought them so I would feel superior, and as shallow as it seemed, it worked. He would say they only wanted to make me upset to break up what we had because they wanted my spot, and I believed him.

I didn't want to be naïve regarding this situation, like in the past. There were no gifts he could buy or money he could give that could erase my pain and embarrassment. This situation was going to be left entirely up to me. I couldn't decide if I should stay and deal with it or move on and live without him.

Chapter Three

Unsure of where I was going or what I was going to do, I left the house and headed down the street to the liquor store to pick up an alcoholic beverage to help ease my pain. I picked up a small bottle of Grey Goose and an Ocean Spray cranberry. I drank half of the juice first then filled the rest of the bottle with the clear liquor. I was truly fucked up over him. My only solution at the moment was to drink my pain away. I couldn't shake him from my mind no matter how hard I tried. Everything I did or thought about at that moment seemed to remind me of Cee and the good ol' days.

Not paying attention to where I was driving, I realized that I had driven over the river and into Kentucky. I parked and chilled at my favorite secluded area by the river and let my tears flow. I couldn't help reminiscing about the good days Cee and I shared. Every time he and I had an altercation, I always managed to make myself feel better by recalling all the good times. Luckily, I managed to retain more good memories than bad.

I thought back to the beginning of our relationship, when Cee offered to take me and my best friend, Shelly, to get some ice cream. He knew the best way to win me over was to get in good graces with my girl, which he did with ease. That day was crazy because we both were looking a hot-ass mess. It was storming outside, so we weren't trying to be cute. We were babysitting for Shelly's cousin, so we weren't paying too much attention to any guys that were trying to get our attention. We would normally smile, wave, and keep it moving.

Shelly was so impressed by Cee's charm and beautiful smile that she threatened to take him from me if I didn't step up. I was familiar with the games guys played, so I read straight through his innocent, charming demeanor. I vowed to make him work to win me over, not the other way around.

Cee was a shy, young hustler without much game, fresh in the streets trying to make it happen for himself. He was nineteen then and I had just turned sixteen. He lied when we first met and told me he was only seventeen. I didn't find out his true age until my mom asked to see his driver's license, which was something I should have done when we first met. He won my mom over with his charm and beautiful smile also, but I wasn't totally convinced.

Problem number one, he didn't own a car. He faithfully drove a different rental car every week. To add insult to injury, his gear was not up to par, so I was not impressed. I played hard to get at first because I knew all the hood hoes wanted him since he was coming up in the game. I, on the other hand, was different, because quietly all of his boys wanted me too, and he knew it.

I finally gave in after Shelly and I almost fought over how stupid I was acting. She and I both knew I was going to lose Cee to another chick if I didn't stop acting immature, so I finally let my guard down and we started kicking it on a regular basis.

I later realized that Cee was very much up in the game and established. He played the low-key role to keep outsiders out of his business. He wasn't the flashy type at all and kept a low profile, which was a good look. I didn't like people in my business, and now, with a baller, I damn sure didn't want people speculating and being nosy.

The low profile didn't last long once he knew he had locked me in and officially had me on his team. I was a stunna all by myself, so he knew he had to do everything within his power to keep me intrigued and happy. Even if it meant blinging a little and being flashy every now and then. I appreciated and admired the way he was willing to step it up a notch for me.

I remember the first time he came to pick me up from my mom's house in a shiny green Corvette. I was impressed because he had excelled past the monthly rentals and purchased a car of his own. He had also stepped his jewelry game up by buying a shiny diamond cross, which hung low on his muscular chest. I was definitely impressed by his new look.

He messed my head up when I got in the car and noticed he had a stack of money bound in a thick rubber band sitting in the passenger seat. When I tried to give it to him he told me it was mine to pamper myself with. I was surprised that I didn't even have to ask. I was very impressed by his generosity. Inside, I was screaming like a little schoolgirl, but on the outside, I played it cool like it was nothing.

I was a little nervous when he took me to his apartment for the first time. Surprisingly, his place was decorated nicely for a young single man. Everything was black and silver, all the way down to his appliances. The soft tunes of Dru Hill's, *Somebody's Sleeping in My Bed* filled the room as he proved his cooking skills in the kitchen. He prepared homemade lasagna, tossed salad, and garlic bread. I had to admit, the entire night was very relaxing and romantic.

I watched him attentively and admired his every move as he fluidly prepared our meal. Something about being around him made me comfortable; I felt special. I laughed a genuine laugh whenever he told a joke, and my heart smiled whenever he would wink his eye or blow me random kisses. I was happy with him, and made up my mind that night. With him is where I wanted to be. We exclusively dated and spent almost every day together after our first date, sharing laughs and good times. I appreciated how he never pressed me for sex until I was ready to take that next step. I was blessed that I had scored a true gentleman.

Those were the golden days that I cherished and missed the most. After about two wonderful years, I began to notice my dazzling days growing into depressing lonely nights.

* * * *

Lost in the memories of the past and in the dismal moment at hand, I realized that two hours had rapidly passed. I was halfway intoxicated, and relaxed enough to return home and face reality. I parked in front of the house, slumped down in the seat of my car, and found myself once again lost in thought of what was to come of this situation. I stared at the front door, unsure of what would occur once I went in.

After stirring up enough courage, I slowly approached the door, jingling my keys loudly to alert him that I was home. Strangely, after unlocking my door, I stepped into an eerily quiet house. Immediately, I ran upstairs to see if he had put his things back in the closet, but to my dismay, the bags that I had previously filled were all removed from the house. Everything was gone, even personal items I hadn't touched. I slowly stomped down the steps, defeated, feeling lost, stupid, and upset. *What had I done now?* I plopped down on my sofa, took another swig of my drink, and relaxed my head on the pillow. As I closed my eyes, the buildup of burning tears barged their way through my swollen eyelids and flowed as freely as the Nile.

I never thought he would actually leave, not without a fight anyway. I was looking forward to coming home to him waiting for me in the bed, with all his clothes back in their original places. I wanted him to beg and plead for my forgiveness, but he was nowhere in sight. My baby was gone, and once again I was all alone.

I was confused. Who was at fault here? Was I wrong for lashing out the way I did? Was I wrong for hurting and seeking remorseful arms to console my pain? He was the one who had cheated and deceived me, not the other way around. I needed answers and he held the key.

Nervously, I punched the numbers into the phone as I called his cell and patiently waited for him to answer. Luckily, I got his voicemail. I wasn't really ready to talk nor had I thoroughly thought through what I wanted to say or prepared a speech. Growing with rage from being ignored, I hung up and called again. The same thing, no answer. My feelings were crushed. I sucked up my pain and anger, then called the one person who always knew Cee's whereabouts.

"Hey, Ms. Marie. Have you seen Cee?" I asked, trying to sound as normal as possible, now pacing back and forth.

"Yeah, he was here about two hours ago. He came by and dropped off some bags. How did it go today?"

"Not good at all. I lost my cool." I was sad all over again, thinking about our earlier altercation. "I'm sorry, Ms. Marie, I have to go. I have another call coming in," I said, rushing her off the phone, hoping it was Cee calling me back.

"Okay, if I talk to him, I'll tell him you called."

"Thanks, Marie. Bye."

"Hello," I answered anxiously, without bothering to look at the caller I.D.

"Hey, Ree!" My loud, obnoxious friend Shelly screamed into the phone.

Annoyed, I yelled so she could hear me over the music blaring in the background. "Where you at?"

"At The Palace. Girl, Cee is up in here with his boys and some hoes in VIP. Why ain't you here?"

"Oh, I'm on my way," I said, as my blood began to boil and my heart began to race. No reason for me to be up in the house crying, all sad and shit, while this fool was out partying with hoes. Oh hell no!

"Shelly, tell Pete to meet me at the door in an hour, and call me immediately if Cee or those hoes try anything stupid. Okay?"

"I got you, girl. You know I'm on it. Here's Pete. I'll tell him now. See you when you get here," Shelly yelled, and hung up.

My clothes couldn't come off fast enough. I snatched everything off and ran into to the bathroom to take a quick shower. With the towel wrapped around my dripping wet body, I searched my closet for something simple yet cute to wear. Deciding on the new gold and black BEBE outfit Cee recently bought for me, I briskly applied some lotion and ran back into the bathroom to flat iron my hair. I lightly applied some mascara, eyeliner, powder foundation, and made sure my lip gloss was popping with my "Oh Baby" Mac lip gloss. I sprayed on Cee's favorite, *J'adore* by Christian Dior, slid on my stilettos, and was out.

20

Chapter Four

When I arrived at the club, my boy Pete was already posted at the door waiting for me. Without hesitation, he escorted me right in. I breezed by everybody I knew because I was on a mission to see what Cee was up to and wasn't in the mood for petty chitchat. I stormed straight over to the VIP section, and sure enough, there he was, posted with a pack of chicks lingering around.

I stayed off to the side of the VIP so he wouldn't notice me right away. I wanted to see just how he behaved without me around. After about ten minutes of watching him do a whole bunch of nothing, my patience began wearing thin, so I decided to make my presence known.

"What the fuck are you doing here, Cee?" I asked, hovering over him as he poured himself a drink. He was surrounded by his regular crew and some random females. He had the nerve to be all giggling and smiling up in other people's faces like nothing ever happened a few hours ago.

"What you doing here?" He asked nonchalantly, better yet, like he really didn't care.

"Who the fuck are these hoes and why are they up here in your space?" I asked, standing directly in front of him, pointing to the three random females sitting too close to him who were now grinning and whispering amongst themselves, enjoying the scene.

I couldn't believe he had the audacity to just sit there and do me like this, like we were just regular acquaintances and not a couple. I'm the one he put through the drama, and he had the nerve to sit there all stone faced and ask what I was doing there, like I wasn't welcome.

"Who are you calling a ho?" The chick closest to Cee asked smartly. She actually was the cutest of the three. She was a light brown, slender girl, and wore a short Halle Berry haircut. Her makeup was simple, yet her mouth was fly. She was exactly his type. "We up here 'cause he asked us to come up here."

I cut my eyes at the loose-lipped female. "Seriously bitch, kill the noise already!" I waved her off and rolled my eyes with fury. My main concern was my man. I directed my attention back to Cee, who had his head turned talking to some guy, paying me no mind. I had no energy to entertain these miscellaneous broads.

"Come with me," I growled between clenched teeth, grabbing Cee's arm.

"For what? You kicked me out, remember?" he replied sarcastically, yanking his arm back.

"Oh, so you showing out now 'cause you got a little audience. Huh? Well, laugh at this."

Boldly, I threw the entire bucket of ice that was sitting on the table on Cee and the chick sitting next to him. Cee, the chick, and all of her friends jumped up, stunned from my reaction. Everyone else sat around looking shocked as well from witnessing me act out like that in public. He wasn't going to embarrass me like I was nothing to him; he had to be taught a lesson.

Shelly had her eye on me the entire time and was already posted at the bottom of the VIP, ready for anyone to act like they were going to put their hands on me. As soon as they all stood up, Shelly was standing directly beside me with Pete behind her.

"You know what, Cee? Fuck you!" I screamed with my heart beating a mile a minute in my chest, both scared of his reaction and upset that he had me in such a bad mental space to even do something as stupid as this. "You can have these low-class hoes. Since you doing you, I'm gonna do me." I stormed away, piping mad with Shelly and Pete in tow.

I made my rounds in the club, dancing a little with every step I took, looking for someone familiar to dance with or to occupy my time. I wanted to piss Cee off just like I was and make him jealous for a change. I danced alone and scanned the floor for about fifteen minutes, but unfortunately none of the guys that approached me came remotely close to being on Cee's level. He was in a league of his own, especially in my eyes.

I ended up going to the other side of the club with Shelly and her friend, Angelica. I really didn't deal with Shelly's people because they were always in my business trying to find out what was what and gossiping about who they heard was messing with who. I heard that my name and Cee's was in Angelica's mouth a time or two. She made it her business to know everybody business, but was careful not to let any rumors slip out around me or Shelly. However, tonight I didn't care. I sat there with the girls, laughing, dancing, and giggling, waiting for Cee to come over and make some sort of a scene. I knew he was pissed off and wasn't going to let my little stunt slide that easy. The countdown began as I sat there anxiously, waiting for him to come over and let me have it.

About fifteen minutes later, Cee came through the door and asked the bouncer where I was. The burly guy immediately pointed in my direction like a snitch in the streets. I watched him attentively, step by step, as he made his way over to our table. His eyes were narrowed and his lips were tight; he was pissed! He had taken off his soaked shirt and was down to his wife-beater, showing off all his milk chocolate, beautiful muscles. Over and over I whispered to myself, "*Stay focused Desiree, stay focused.*"

"Let's go, Desiree," Cee said angrily, snatching me up by my arm like I was a rag doll.

Shelly looked at me like, *bitch, you gonna let him jack you up like that*, but kept her mouth shut, because she didn't want to get involved with no mess between me and Cee.

"For what? Where your hoes at?" I asked, trying to snatch my arm away. Shelly and I began laughing nervously.

"I said let's go; your little show is over. I don't see shit funny. You up in here wildin' out, making a scene in the club and shit. Let's go!" he yelled, jerking my arm harder.

"Don't you see me chilling with my girls, having a good old time? We're doing us like you were doing you." I had to keep my composure and play the tough role even through the tears that were welling up behind my eyes and from the pain of him yanking on my arm. He had to pay for the drama and embarrassment he was putting me through. He needed to realize he could be replaced with no problem.

Before I knew it, Cee slapped the apple martini out my hand and roughly snatched me up from my seat. Shelly and Angelica both sat there silent and shocked with their eyes wide. They had never seen Cee angry at me or act out of character in public.

A little force was all it took for him to drag me out the club. It was crazy. People were watching like I was getting dragged out by the police, but I was loving every minute of it. Someone had already pulled his car around and had it parked out front, engine running and ready. He opened the passenger door of his Benz and shoved me in. He got in the car, stared at me for a minute; obviously fuming in rage, shook his head, and sped off, causing me to jerk back in my seat.

From the club, he silently drove to IHOP to get some breakfast before it got too crowded with the rush of partygoers from various clubs. I wasn't hungry, but he clearly didn't care because he never asked if I wanted anything to eat. He got out the car, slammed the door shut, and went in to order his food.

Apparently, he was so lost in his thoughts and consumed with anger that he accidently left his cell phone in the car. Curiosity burned through me with every second that passed. I wondered and contemplated taking the chance to see what I could find in his phone. Nervously, I looked from the phone to him, back to the phone, and then again to him. I picked up the phone, held it low, and unlocked his code. I was all in it, checking how many voicemail messages and text messages there were, trying to find anything I could. I could hear my heart as it raced and thumped nervously in my chest, terrified I was going to get caught.

Cee didn't play about me snooping through his things. He always said I snooped because I wanted to find something, and if he caught me, he would intentionally have something in there for me to look at. At times he acted like he was my father or something, and not my companion. But, he made his point, because I didn't look through anything. I never knew when it could be a possible set up.

I knew he hadn't had a chance to erase or hide anything since I interrupted his night, so this was perfect timing. I searched to see if there were any numbers I didn't recognize that could possibly be this unknown baby's momma. However, before I could finish my investigation and remember or store any unfamiliar numbers in my phone, he started walking back toward the car. Quickly, I shut off the phone, put it back in its original spot, folded my arms across my chest, and slapped a mean mug on my face.

"What's wrong with you, Desi?" Cee calmly asked. "This shit has to stop. You wildin' out in the club and shit. I don't need this kind of drama."

Underneath my anger was a slight grin because he was hot and my mission was accomplished. I needed him to feel the pain I was feeling, and what better way than to show out in public. He hated that.

"It wouldn't be a scene or drama if you weren't posted up in there with those bitches. How would you feel if I told you I was pregnant and the baby wasn't yours, then ran to the club with Shelly partying and shit? You wouldn't be so happy, now would you?"

"Man, look, I said I'm sorry. Now let's squash this shit. What do you want me to do? I admitted it, told you the truth, and yeah, I was wrong. I messed up by not being honest from the jump, I'm sorry, and I'm coming back home tonight, too. We can discuss this further when you calm your ass down and can think rationally."

"Think rationally my ass! Fuck being rational. I'm pissed off!" I cried. "And if you're coming home, why did you take your stuff to your mom's house?"

"Because you packed up all my clothes. I wasn't gonna leave it there so you could fuck my shit up, so I took it over there. You wanted me to leave, so I left."

"No, I didn't! What I wanted was for you to be faithful and not take me through anymore hurt and pain, but could you manage to do that? *Nooo*," I replied, being sarcastic.

Cee shook his head. He wasn't getting anywhere talking to me while I was still angry and wasn't going to get his point across any time soon. He left the car, once again slammed the door, and went back inside to pick up his food. There was no way of getting through to him either. He never wanted to understand why he was wrong, and ignoring the situation without communicating our feelings or coming to a solution didn't help anything at all. We needed to talk about this and get everything out in the open so there wouldn't be any more secrets or lies lingering.

He figured everything was okay as long as he had admitted to his wrongdoings, like I was supposed to shut up, accept it, and brush it off like everything was cool. Life was not that simple, and he knew I was not a simple chick. This wasn't the last he was going to hear out of my mouth. Something had to change.

We rode to the house in complete silence. No radio, no conversation, nothing. I was actually too angry to speak to him at this point. All I wanted to do was get home, take a hot shower, pop some Advil, and lay down to rest my throbbing head. We were definitely going to continue this conversation tomorrow after we both had time to cool off and could speak to each other like we had some sense. Maybe then I could get him to see how foul and messed up this situation really was.

Once we got inside the house, I slid out of my clothes, jumped in the shower, and curled up in the bed. Cee finished his food downstairs and wrapped up his conversation with Will on the phone before coming upstairs into our room. When he finally entered the bedroom, he stripped butt-naked, climbed into the bed, and instantly started kissing me roughly, but passionately. I could tell he needed to release some anger, and I was his main target.

"I'll be back," he said, planting a forceful kiss on my belly and playfully mugging me in the head. He walked toward the bathroom singing some song, sounding awful, and turned on the shower.

I knew I didn't have to show out like that in the club, but I was pissed off and felt I needed to once again reclaim my position. I knew what he wanted and I was not at all in the mood. I wanted to remain mad for at least a day or more so he could see I wasn't playing around this time. Cee always felt that sex fixed all our problems and would shut me up. Most of the time, it did. I would shut up for the night, exhausted and tired, but I never let it slip my mind to bring up in the future.

When he returned, he hopped back in the bed, still dripping wet from the water.

"Damn Cee, you getting the bed all wet!" I yelled, irritated, pushing him away from me.

He grabbed me by my waist and yanked me down off my pillows. His juicy lips felt like wet clouds brushing against my warm flesh. My internal temperature suddenly increased with each kiss, and I felt the moisture forming between my thighs from his very touch. Without much resistance, I gave in and started kissing him back with the same amount of passion, which only turned me on more. I loved make-up sex, I couldn't lie, but I was tired of having to go through this just to bypass solving or dealing with our problems.

Lost in the moment, we took our time pleasing each other and aggressively took our frustrations out on each other's bodies. We went round for round, waiting to see who would be the first to give in. He ended the night by passionately caressing and stroking my body with the tips of his fingers, trying to comfort my internal pain. I laid there still and numb, my thighs now saturated. Cee got up and gently wiped me off with a warm, wet hand towel. Silently, as tears flowed down my face, I cried myself to sleep, exhausted both mentally and physically from living my so-called life.

Chapter Five

It seemed like every time we had something major occur in our relationship, we had the ability to brush it all off and act as if nothing had ever happened the morning after good sex. Pitiful, but it was true. Some women have the tendency to forgive and forget too quickly without ever trying to resolve the problem at hand. Like ignoring the situation would make it disappear. We manage to suck it up, mask the issue and our pain with a beautiful fake smile, and keep it moving. That's the reason women are so strong today. We can go through all kinds of hell and hurt with a man, yet somehow manage to keep a fake smile plastered on our faces to keep a happy home.

It's even worse when we can't say anything because he is the sole provider. There's no way we will put our future or stable home in jeopardy by flapping off at the mouth over something dumb, at least dumb to him anyway. Most of the time we know when to shut up, because if we don't know anything else, we know that the quickest way to lose a man's interest is running off at the mouth. Not to get this behavior confused with stupidity, because we are very smart when it comes to reading our men. We know shit. We just don't tell them everything we know. Women always try to stay two steps ahead of the game, at least sometimes.

Over the next few weeks, our relationship went back to normal and continued as if nothing had ever happened. Cee moved all his things back into the house, and the baby situation wasn't brought up again. Not that the thought of the baby didn't poke at my brain every day, I just knew it was useless bringing it up without having further evidence. In my heart, there was no trust for Cee. I was on him like a hawk and tracked his every move whenever he looked like he was up to something suspicious.

Christmas was just a few weeks away, and I was hell-bent on keeping him away from this unknown baby momma and child. I hated to be mean, cruel, or insensitive, but it was what it was, and I felt the way I felt. I wanted him with me and only me, like it had been all along. I came up with a brilliant idea to get him away from the city on Christmas and planned a holiday vacation for just the two of us. We always spent the holidays with his family, but this year, we were going to do something different, just us for a change. I got busy searching for the perfect holiday destination where we could vacation and spend some much needed quality time together. I stayed up for hours on my laptop researching and waiting since Cee hadn't come home yet.

I ended up dozing off with my laptop still on the bed. I was awakened and startled by Cee all up in my face, lying on top of me, cheesing like a Cheshire cat. Through my blurred vision, I glanced at the clock on the nightstand and noticed it was after five o'clock in the morning.

"Good morning, baby," Cee whispered into my ear.

I was pissed that he had the audacity to come in at five o'clock in the morning all chipper, talking about good morning like he had been lying in bed next to me all night.

"Where you been, Cee?" I asked flatly, still half-asleep.

"I got something for you. Sit up," Cee demanded, ignoring my question, kicking off his Timberland boots.

Beginning to get irritated, I turned on my side so I could look at him. "What do you want? I'm sleep and where have you been?"

He then picked up my arm, grabbed my hand, and slid a beautiful diamond ring on my left ring finger. "Is it too loose?" he asked, hovering over me, waiting anxiously to see my reaction toward my new gift.

My excitement made me fully awake and alert. I grinned from ear to ear like I was receiving my first gift on a Christmas morning. "Kind of, but it fits. What's this all about, Cee?" I couldn't take my eyes off the ring; it was stunning.

"It's about us and our future together. It's my promise to you that I will love you and only you forever, so don't ever take it off. You are my world, Desiree, and all the woman that I need. I'm sorry for hurting you in the past, but I promise to make everything right. You have to promise me that you will stick by me through thick and thin, whatever it takes."

Cee spoke with such sincerity and displayed a genuine look of affection on his handsome face. God, I loved this man. I was so consumed by the beautifully crafted ring and overjoyed with excitement that I completely tuned him out. My eyes searched his for anything more that he had to say and was diverted back to the sparkling diamonds; I was in complete disbelief.

"I promise," I said slowly, looking from the ring to the tear that escaped his eye and rolled down his cheek. His eyes never left mine and were piercing through me. I agreed, but at the moment couldn't really comprehend the promise I was making to him.

Where did he get this ring from and how much was it worth? I silently wondered to myself. I would be taking a trip to the local jeweler very soon to confirm the value of this amazing ring that he had blessed me with. I couldn't wait to call Shelly and tell her about my morning surprise. I adjusted myself, fully sat up in the bed, and hugged Cee around his neck as tight as I could, never wanting to let go.

"I have a surprise for you, too," I said, now totally awake and ignoring the fact that he hadn't come in the house all night. At this moment, it didn't even faze me. I was on cloud nine!

"What is it? I know it can't possibly top what's on your left hand," Cee replied, being sarcastic.

"I don't think anything can top that, baby, but I booked us a chalet in Gatlinburg. We leave on the twenty-second."

"That's right before Christmas, Desi."

"I know, but I wanted to do something different this year. Just me and you," I pouted.

Cee stalled and massaged his chin for a minute. I began to worry he was going to decline. He then took hold of my hand and began fondling the ring, moving it from side to side.

"I think that's a great idea baby. I damn sure need to get away for a while. Let me wrap things up with Will and we can leave. Do you need to do some shopping or anything before we leave?"

That was too easy, I thought to myself. "Yeah, just a little. I can pick you up something, too, if you want," I added, batting my eyelashes innocently.

"Yeah, get me some new Timbs, and if you see some fitteds that I'd like, get them too," Cee said as he pulled two wads of money out of his pocket. "Is two enough?"

"Yeah, that's cool. If I go over, I'll pick up the rest. Thank you, baby. I love you."

Cee kissed me on the forehead and left the money on the dresser. Truthfully, I had it made, disregarding all the bullshit that I endured. I didn't care what anybody had to say, my man was good to me, and I wasn't gonna let no baby momma drama ruin that. Even though the ring wasn't a proposal for marriage like I was hoping for, I felt Cee giving me a promise ring was a huge step for us.

To be honest, I was kind of hurt, because I thought he was going to ask me to marry him. I would have immediately screamed yes with no hesitation. Some may think it would be stupid of me to marry him while going through the drama with the baby and all, but I would be just as pleased to jump over my kitchen broom right now if it meant we could tie the knot that easy. I would be willing to take that step and worry about everything else later.

Lost in Love...

I once read a quote that said, "Marriage is like a pair of scissors. Joined in the middle and cannot be easily separated. Often moving in opposite directions, yet always threatening to punish anyone that comes between them." That's exactly how Mr. and Mrs. Thomas were going to be. So, hoes had better watch out, because messing with this relationship could be fatal.

* * * *

Cee knew what Desiree was up to all along, and was kind of happy that she had come up with the idea of taking a vacation for the holidays because he needed to get out of the streets for a while. The streets were getting hotter and hotter by the day, and he didn't feel like having any unnecessary run-ins with the police, and definitely not the feds. So, ducking off for a while would give him some much needed time to cool off and bond with his lady.

He felt bad that he wouldn't be there for his little man's first Christmas, because he had been there for him since he was born. Terra knew exactly what she was doing when she got pregnant. He gave her the money to abort the baby, but she declined, saying she didn't believe in abortions. She figured she had hit the jackpot with Cee, but he refused to let her use him by throwing the kid in his face all the time.

Whenever Terra allowed him to spend quality time with little Darius, he grew more and more attached and cared for him immensely. He wanted to be in his life every step of the way, but getting Desiree on board with the whole idea was an entire different story. Cee wasn't the type of man to conceive a child and leave the kid or the mother hanging, no matter what his circumstances were or who he was with. He couldn't understand how guys these days could have random children in the streets and not take care of them, or at least want to see them grow up.

"What's up, Will? I need to holla at you for a minute," Cee said after placing a call to his right-hand man while sitting in his Benz, flipping through his CD case looking for his Notorious Big *Life After Death* CD. He was in that type of mood.

"What's up, man?"

"Me and Desiree are gonna take a little trip for Christmas. So, I'm gonna need you to hold it down for me until I get back, and pick up some toys and shit for my little man."

"That's cool. When y'all leaving?" Will asked as he finished putting the last touches on his freshly rolled blunt, lighting the tip with his initialed chrome lighter, one of his many birthday gifts he had received from Cee last year.

"On the twenty-second. I'll give you a couple stacks to fuck with. Spend the majority on Darius and give Terra the rest."

Will took a long draw of the potent marijuana and began to speak between raspy coughs. "So, what should I tell her when she ask me why I'm dropping off the toys instead of you?"

"You don't have to tell her shit. It ain't none of her business. Just give her the money and she'll be cool. That will keep her hungry ass quiet for a minute."

"All right, I got you, bro. You still coming through today, right?" Will asked, coughing, trying to clear his throat.

"Yeah, I'll be through. I gave my baby the ring today, she happy as hell too."

"So when y'all getting married?" Will asked as he pounded on his chest, laughing and coughing at the same time.

"After I find out about Darius. Terra is tripping about this paternity test, like I shouldn't have doubts about Darius. I just made a promise to Desiree to hold her over. That was the best I could do for now. I'm not making any commitments with all this lingering in the air. Anyway, what your ass want for Christmas?" Cee asked, changing the subject, because the thought of Terra always seemed to piss him off.

"You ain't even got to ask. You already know."

"I got you when I get back brotha. One."

Cee ended his call, then adjusted the volume and bass on his stereo system. With the sudden news of this spur-of-the-moment trip, he knew he needed to try and wrap up the streets the best he could before he departed for his vacation. He had to make sure he left his guys with enough work in the streets so everyone could have a Merry Christmas.

Chapter Six

The vacation was everything I could have asked for and more, simply beautiful and peaceful. We met the cutest couple that was staying in the chalet next door to ours. He was white and she was a fierce Spanish chick. They were celebrating their first wedding anniversary and asked us to join in on the celebration. I couldn't believe Cee actually agreed to hanging with them, because he didn't vibe with strangers at all. I had to admit they were mad fun.

Somehow, spending time and speaking with them about their undeniable love made Cee and I bond over the trip. We paraded around with them like we were also a happily married couple. We took a tour of the Smokey Mountains together and ate lunch at a very classy restaurant. The way the couple communicated and interacted with each other inspired me. Cee and I fed off their positive energy and took notes on their affirmative nature.

We shared good times with the couple and also spent quality time in our chalet, bonding and talking about our future together. We cooked together, played cards, and shot some strip pool, which ended with me shooting my last ball butt-naked. My real reason for planning the getaway was completely forgotten once I realized how much fun we were having together. This was the first time we were alone away from everyone and everything on a major holiday, and I actually appreciated the serenity of it all.

After our trip, I realized we were going to be okay together. That is, until something managed to get in our way.

* * * *

We had agreed to leave our phones off until we arrived back in the city, so we wouldn't have any distractions, but as soon as we touched down from the airport, Cee's phone beeped continuously with voicemail alerts, vibrated with missed text messages, and calls came in incessantly. Exhausted after returning all the calls I had missed while we were away, I was in desperate need of taking a nap. It seemed like more people called while you were away than when they knew you were at home bored to death.

Cee left immediately after dropping me off at home. He said things had gotten wild while we were away, so he had to go discuss some issues that came up with Will. I guess the streets didn't know what to do with him gone for a whole week.

Really needing to unwind before unpacking and cooking dinner, I cut all the calls I returned short. I was glad Cee had left the house for a while because I was growing tired of having him all up in my face every minute. Cee was a very affectionate person and I loved that about him, but sometimes it became overwhelming and totally nerve-racking.

After my nap, which ended up being about three hours worth of sleep, I began unpacking our things and hung up all the unnecessary new clothes we had purchased at the shopping centers. We had brought back so much stuff it was ridiculous. I bought Shelly and Marie back some things to make up for our absence on Christmas. I knew Marie was upset at us, because she never spent a holiday without seeing her son, but if he and I were going to get married, a lot of things were going to have to change.

I took some ground beef out of the freezer to thaw for tonight's dinner to go along with the homemade mashed potatoes, corn, and cabbage that I was going to prepare for my man. He had been out ever since we got home, and I knew he would be hungry and irritated when he returned. I figured why not treat him to a home cooked meal after our wonderful vacation. He deserved it. Besides, I needed to start playing my position if I planned on staying in the game.

Around 9:45 p.m., as I pulled the meatloaf out of the oven, there was a knock at the back door by the kitchen. I had no clue who it could be at the door without notice. We rarely had visitors, and when we did, they certainly did not use the back door to gain entry to our home. I quietly walked to the door and looked through the peephole to see who it could possibly be at this hour.

There stood a tall, slender, caramel-colored chick freezing in the cold, blowing air into her hands in an attempt to warm them. She had a long, straight black weave that hung over the front of her white pea coat. She was a nice-looking girl, but I was confused as to what she was knocking on my door for? I watched her for a minute as she jitterly moved around, looking back and forth like a crackhead waiting for her next fix. I swung the door open with a nasty attitude because we didn't have unannounced visitors, and especially not females.

"Can I help you?" I asked, with one hand on my hip and the other still on the doorknob, careful not to let too much cold air seep into the house.

"Oh...um...um...I'm sorry. I must have the wrong address," the young girl stuttered while staring at me like a deer in bright headlights. She stood there frozen, not from the cold, but obviously shocked to see me on the other side of the door, and remained incoherent.

"Well what address were you looking for?" I asked, breaking the silence, trying not to intimidate the girl.

I tried to come off half-way polite, but I guess it didn't work because the girl actually took off running down the street like I started shooting at her or something. I stood there in complete shock, shaking my head, totally confused.

"What the hell!" I said aloud, standing there confused and amused as I watched the chick run halfway down the street before hopping into the passenger side of a silver Ford Explorer, which sped away into the night.

After the truck was out of sight, I just stood there in total disbelief. I didn't know what to think; this was way too weird. Yes, this girl could have indeed had the wrong address, but something told me this was not by mistake. My intuition instantly informed me who this chick was. She was either trying to make herself known or was hoping that Cee was the one who greeted her at the door. A woman's intuition can be a bitch, but this bitch on the other side of my door was bold!

I didn't mention anything to Cee when he came in that night. I was actually hoping the girl would come back, so I could lure her into the house to interrogate the hell out of her for information. During dinner, I could hardly pay attention to Cee as he rambled on about his day and ran down the plans for the New Year's party. My mind was too far gone thinking about all the *what ifs*, if she was to ever return.

After dinner, I tried on my new outfits for him, strutting my stuff up and down our hallway like a runway model, all while he counted his day's profits. I later became his sweet dessert.

* * * *

New Years was just a couple of hours away, and Will was throwing the ultimate New Year's bash at The Palace. Of course, Cee and I got fresh to death, because we were making our first public appearance together after the last incident at the club. I especially had to be on my finest because I knew that hoes would be

44

thinking Cee and I wouldn't be together after our last altercation. So, I had to let them know I wasn't at all replaceable, not this year anyway.

I wore a sexy, knee-length dress I had ordered from French Connection that hung off my shoulder and was cut into a low V in the back. Yeah, it was too chilly for the dress, but I was hot to death. My footwear for the night consisted of a simple pair of silver Jimmy Choo pumps that were too high and were killing my feet already. Still, I managed to stomp it out like a model anyway. A girl's got to do what a girl's got to do. I even had my hair stylist, Tasha, roll my hair in large rollers and pull it all to the side so I could have the classic Marilyn Monroe curls going on.

I decided to put on my diamond necklace and matching bracelet Cee had bought for me last Christmas. I rarely wore it except for around Cee, because I was too scared someone would try to snatch it from around my neck. After getting my ring appraised, I had the jeweler shine it up nice so I would be shining for everyone to see. I intentionally waved my left hand around every chance I got, so everyone could notice the new huge rock on my ring finger, and think that Cee and I were now engaged.

Cee wore a simple, black Armani button-down top and matching pants that had a vintage look to them with these crazy designs and stitching on the back pockets. I was pleased that he decided to wear his custom-made, white gold initial cufflinks that I had designed for his birthday last year. Him wearing the cuff links made me happy, because I didn't think he really liked them since he had only worn them once before tonight.

His wrist game complimented his "GQ" style perfectly. The diamonds on his freshly polished bracelets reflected like two strobe lights attached to his wrists. On one arm, he wore his Breitling watch that he had brought back from his Los Angeles trip and a simple, black diamond bracelet. The other wrist was adorned with the three-carat diamond bracelet that he wore with everything. He made sure to get a fresh shape up that morning, so the waves in his hair were jumping and on point. He felt the need to complement me the same way I felt I needed to complement him, and I loved that. We were ready to stunt on all of the haters that would be in attendance, waiting to see who was wearing what and who came with who.

Cee purchased some new chrome rims for his snow-white Range, which went together perfectly. This was the first time he brought the truck out after he had the rims put on, so people instantly thought he had bought himself a new whip for the new year. We were definitely rolling as hot as we looked.

Cee valet parked the truck, so all of the people in line could get a good look at us and talk amongst themselves about who was hopping out of the *cocaine range*. Cee had clout in the city. Therefore, people usually only stared and complimented, but never disrespected or hated in his presence. Cee insisted on helping me out the truck like a gentlemen instead of the valet man that rushed to my side. He didn't do this on the regular, so I knew he was showing off, and I was loving every minute of it.

Cee gave dap to a couple of the people lingering around outside of the packed club, and I saw a couple of girls that I knew from my old hood standing in the line, desperately trying to get my attention so they could enter the club with me. They wanted to be able to say they were with me and Cee so they could get out of the freezing cold weather. I kept my arm interlocked with Cee's while he casually talked to his boys. I smiled politely and listened attentively to Cee's conversation, trying to ignore the girls that were constantly screaming my name like we were friends. Eventually, I waved to the chicks in the line, smiled a fake smile, and kept it moving.

We walked straight inside the club and exchanged greetings with the club managers and bouncers. After saying our casual hellos, Cee looked over his guest list and was guided to his favorite VIP section by the manager of the club. The VIP was already set up with various liquors, champagne, and juices. Almost immediately, even before we could take our seats, a waitress came over, pouring us complementary glasses of Ace of Spades champagne from the club owner. The managers knew exactly what Cee liked and catered to my boo, because they knew they would be graciously taken care of at the end of the night. The three of us cheered to having a great night and a blessed New Year. Once I spotted Shelly over by the bar talking to Pete and another bouncer, I excused myself and went over to say hello.

"What up, chick?" I yelled with a cheesy smile, took a step back to check her out, and embraced her in our usual best friend hug.

It's funny how we behaved once spotting each other in the club. I had just seen Shelly yesterday, but let something be going on like a special event or outing, and we acted like we hadn't seen each other in months.

Shelly managed to squeeze her thick, round frame into a mini, gray, scoop neck Guess sweater dress that made her double D breasts look like two round melons sitting on top of her chest. Shelly was by far fat. She would be considered the thick, voluptuous type that was proportioned just right.

She wore the black Steve Madden knee-high boots that I had brought her back from my Gatlinburg trip, which hugged her thick legs perfectly. Every strand in her hair was laid, compliments of our wonderful stylist Tasha. With Shelly's every move, the large, shiny curls of her roller wrap bounced along right with her. My girl was looking fierce. She could definitely give the females in here a run for their money if they tried to look at her like she was anything but fly.

"What up, Pete?" I asked, lightly punching him on his large, muscular arm and giving him a friendly hug.

"Girl, you look like the bomb. I'm loving that dress, bitch!" Shelly yelled while spinning me around and checking me out. "Girl, let me tell you, Pete was just asking me where you were because some chick was at the door arguing back and forth about how she was with Cee and Will and needed to be let in the VIP. They wouldn't let her in because her name wasn't on the list, and neither Will or Cee wasn't here to vouch for her. The girl was out there tripping hard like she was family or something," Shelly rambled.

"Who was she, Pete, and what did she have on?" I asked, trying to find out more information about this mysterious chick.

"Shit, I don't know. She be up in here all the time. She has to be under twenty-one, though, because she be wearing a black band around her wrist. Probably just another thirsty ass female trying to come up off someone else's man," Pete said, bashing the girl in his deep, sexy, raspy voice.

"Show me who she is," I bluntly stated, ready to see if I knew this girl or not.

"I will when I see her again. Simmer down, Rambo." Pete laughed at my eagerness to know who this girl was. "I'll be working the door for a while, and she'll have to come through me to get in. They sent her back to the regular line 'cause she couldn't get in VIP, so she'll be there for a while. I'll come find you when she comes back in. You want me let her on this side if she tries to come through again?"

"Yeah, let her through. We'll see who she really wants," I said, ready for something to pop off.

Shelly and I walked back our VIP section where a couple of guys and their groupies had joined Cee. I had to be the ringleader of the group and cordially introduce myself, so everyone would know who I was.

"How is everyone doing? I'm Desiree, Cee's girl, and this is my best friend, Shelly. If anyone needs anything, don't hesitate to let me know," I added, being way too extra.

Cee laughed out loud and pulled me down on his lap. I loved it when my man showed public affection, especially in the club. The night was going so well that I had actually forgotten about the mystery chick. A couple local acts performed, and Will had booked Jim Jones come and headline the event, which really got the party started. Everyone was drinking, eating, and some even blazed up some of that good, which reeked and clouded up the entire VIP. Even though it was cloudy and you could barely breathe normal air, everyone stayed seated and took advantage of the contact, even if they didn't smoke. I was starting to feel my buzz a little too much after drinking the champagne, two Apple Martinis, a Goose and cranberry, and two tequila shots. I slowed down and drank a couple of bottled waters so I could keep my composure and remain level-headed, just in case anything was to go down.

Shelly and I were winding our bodies and singing *Party* by Beyoncé to each other, when Will stood up and started whispering something in Cee's ear. Shelly and I both looked at each other and giggled, while sipping on our drinks, dancing, and tripping off Will.

Will always rocked the same type of attire everyday no matter what was going on. Will was the small, lanky type that wore clothes too big for his small frame. He either wore a collared polo or thermal-type shirt with no design or anything, just bland. His pants were always baggy and hung low around his slim waist. He owned every pair of Timberlands that hit the shelves, and tonight, he threw on his traditional wheats with a caramel thermal and an army fatigue Polo vest. He was the straight New York type of nigga and didn't tolerate any unnecessary bullshit either. I appreciated him for being the loyal friend he was to Cee, because through hell and high water, he was always there no matter what.

Cee and Will were like night and day when it came to style, but when it came down to business, they connected like a lock and key. Cee's mother raised Will after his mother died in an automobile accident when he was thirteen, and she had treated him like he was her biological son ever since. Cee and Will always claimed to be brothers and even resembled each other a little after they grew into men.

Will and I didn't click when Cee and I first started dating, because I think he was jealous that Cee and I were spending so much time together. He must have thought I was taking his boy from him and not allowing him to do the things they used to do before I came into the picture. After he realized I wasn't going anywhere, and I wasn't just another thirsty chick trying to trap his boy, he opened up and got to know me. After we bonded and he started hanging out with us, I became like a little sister-in-law to him.

Will continued talking to Cee, who responded with a shocked, angry look on his face and immediately stood up to follow behind Will. They stopped at the steps to the entrance of the VIP and exchanged words with some of the other guys that were standing around. Will left the little entourage, rushed over to the area of the dance floor that was directly across from our VIP, and yanked someone up by their arm.

I couldn't get a good look at what was going on or who he was jacking up because of the large crowd that was forming around them. I gave Shelly the eye for her to go peep the scene to see what was going on out there. Shelly, who was already on it, headed down the steps to the dance floor without me having to say a word. That girl could read my thoughts like we had mental telepathy or like we were blood sisters. Either way, the girl had my back. She stood close by Will and started winding her body seductively so she could eavesdrop and cop a feel. Will and Shelly both had a crush on each other, but neither would make a move because Shelly's old man, Mark, was Will's right-hand man before he got locked up. Therefore, they kept it cool.

After about five minutes, Shelly ran over to me out of breath, but still trying to play it cool. "Bitch, Will is hot! He was asking the bouncers how did that chick get over here. That's when Cee came down and got instantly mad, too, like he knew the girl. They told security to kick her out because she was too young to be over here anyway," Shelly excitedly informed me as she ran of breath. We stood and watched the scene from the steps.

Shelly loved to gossip and was always on point to let me know if there was any drama with my man or his crew. Before she could finish, there was commotion and a crowd forming around Cee and Will. All I could see was a bouncer handling some chick that was wild'n out, kicking and screaming. Shelly and I rushed over to see what was going on and who this girl was causing a scene. I went and stood directly by Cee, locking my arm in his.

"Go back up there, baby, before it gets crazy out here. I don't want you around this ghetto shit," Cee demanded, trying to push me away.

"I'm cool. You're out here, so I'm okay," I replied straight-faced, standing my ground by his side.

My eyes were glued and never left the familiar face that I was immediately drawn to after Cee spoke to me. I suddenly realized the chick who was causing all the commotion was the same chick who had showed up at my house that night. She must have felt some kind of way when she noticed that I was now standing by my man, and calmed down.

Will went over to the girl and the bouncer that had her jacked up, and tried his best to try and diffuse the situation. Whatever Will said to the girl must have worked, because the bouncer let her go. She regained her composure and stood there, straightening her clothes out and looking embarrassed and very upset.

She must have been dazed or disoriented, because she started walking in me and Cee's direction.

"Where the fuck were you on Christmas, Cee?" The girl yelled, pointing in Cee's face with tears in her eyes.

I stepped in between the girl and Cee with my arms folded, shielding my man. "Hold up, hoe! He was with me, where he was supposed to be, so it's best you back the fuck up!"

"Well, he should have taken his son right along with you then if it was all like that," the girl said, putting emphasis on 'you' as she spoke directly to me. "Darius was up all night crying, Cee. My baby's first fucking Christmas and you were with this bitch!"

The girl continued to try and speak to Cee around me as I stood there with my feet planted.

"If this is your child's first Christmas, he's too young to have any idea what is going on. You need to get up out of here with this stupid shit you on. Don't come up in here with this bullshit, ruining our night. I'm sorry you're a single mother and all, and in need of a baby daddy, but you need to find another one 'cause this one is mines, hoe."

I must have cut the girl to the core and shattered any hopes and dreams that she may have had, because the bitch hauled off and punched me dead in the face.

Not even a split-second went by before I could react or focus, when I saw a Moet bottle come crashing down over her head. I stood there in shock, covering my mouth, looking at the hopeless girl sprawled out on the dance floor submerged in blood and bubbly champagne. It seemed like everything came to a sudden halt as people gathered around looking to see what had happened.

"Clean up on the dance floor," the DJ announced, and the crowd roared out in laughter. He then blasted the song *Fuck Them Other Niggas*. Everyone sang along and got the party back jumpin' again like nothing had ever happened.

Cee grabbed me by the arm and rushed me out of the club. I didn't even have to wonder who did the damage or why. I already knew who. My ride-or-die Shelly was a true goon and down for whatever when it came to her girls.

We swiftly exited the club and headed to an afterhours spot that Will's stepfather owned before the police showed up. We all stuck together the rest of the night until the wee hours of the morning, having a good time laughing, drinking, and kicking it. Even though we had a major disturbance that night, we decided to write it off with the rest of the bullshit that occurred that year.

I made a toast with my friends and agreed to let the petty drama disappear with the passing year. However, in the back of my mind, I knew this situation was far from over. The never-ending drama for my New Year was just getting started.

Chapter Seven

The very next day, I went and pressed harassment and assault charges on the girl for coming to my house and punching me in my face. I figured it would be the most civil thing to do before the situation got too far out of hand. I fabricated most of the information I gave to add a little more excitement to her charges. I knew the restraining order would at least scare this tramp enough to keep her away from Cee if I couldn't. I found out from my hairdresser that the chick's name was Terra Alexander and she was only nineteen years old. To make matters worse, she lived about three minutes from my house, down the block and around the corner.

Shelly had done some damage to the girl, but didn't get in any trouble because no one could prove who had hit her with the bottle. The chick ended up having to get stitches in her head that would for sure leave an ugly scar once healed. I smirked at the thought, because this way, she'd think twice before trying to fuck with me, my crew, or my man. Thankfully, she didn't have any brain damage, because I needed her to be able to remember every detail of her and Cee's relationship once I got a hold of her.

Pete told the police some fools were acting crazy in the club and in the midst of the commotion threw a bottle, accidently hitting her in the head. I guess someone must have bribed her not to press any charges, because if she didn't know before now, she was messing with some true psycho bitches.

Once I obtained Terra's address and information, I was geared up, ready to start my investigation and prepare my stakeouts. I didn't mention anything that I had found out about Terra to Cee, because I wanted him to follow his regular routine without suspecting I was up to anything unusual. If he was still messing around with her, I was going to find out for myself. I was trained on how to be a snoop at an early age when my mom had me breaking into my father's house, trying to catch him cheating on her, which was a regular occurrence. It was sad what all I had to go through as a child and how it affected me now as an adult.

A couple days into my investigation, there was no activity. Cee came in on time and volunteered his whereabouts every conversation we had. I had no job or hobby, so that meant I had too much time on my hands to worry about what he was doing. I rode past the girl's house about three times a day for GP (general purposes) and made it a point to breeze by whenever I had to go somewhere or when I returned home. The girl had a big, black Chow dog that stayed outside, so I couldn't snoop around like I wanted to.

I laid off for a couple of days so nothing would look suspicious, until one night, Cee kept saying he was on his way home every time I called. It was now two-thirty in the morning and I was getting beyond fed up with waiting and hearing his excuses. I couldn't take it anymore, so I decided to get out of bed and hit the streets. Both of his cars were parked on the street, so I knew he couldn't be too far. I gave him the benefit of the doubt and rode around the corner to Will's house first before heading to where I was really itching to go. It's funny how females can trick ourselves into believing what we want to believe when we really know the truth. All of the lights were out at Will's house, and his girl's Camry was parked behind his in the driveway, so I knew Cee wasn't there.

I wanted to know the truth, but wasn't ready to accept it. If he was still cheating, what would I do? Leave again? I don't think so. I was not about to make it that easy for a another female to come and take my spot. I had to ease my mind and find out what was really going on, because Cee damn sure wasn't about to volunteer any more information regarding this situation.

I parked my car on the corner where the girl lived, and waited patiently. The same Ford Explorer that she hopped in when she fled from my house pulled up, and it looked like four teenagers got out, two girls and two guys. I sighed with relief when I noticed neither of the guys were Cee. I sat silently in my car, watching as the couples hugged and kissed in the freezing cold thinking to myself, *the kids these days.*

All of a sudden, a full-figured woman approached the door in a petticoat, holding a baby in her arms. She stood behind the screen door and screamed, "Get in here! Do y'all know what time it is?" She was so loud that I could hear her from where I was parked on the corner.

I'm not sure if a person's heart can actually sink into their stomach, but my heart did just that when I saw Cee walk up to the lady from behind and kiss the little baby on his face. He then went into his pocket, pulled out a wad of money, gave it to the lady, and rubbed the kid on its head. I was sick.

"Son of a bitch!" I said aloud. I called his cell right then to see if he would answer while in the presence of these people. He looked at his cell, pressed the button to send me to voicemail, and put the phone back in his pocket. The boys that were outside with their girlfriends must have been Terra's brothers, because they slowly headed up the steps as the two girls started to walk away.

Cee gave dap to both of the boys and swiftly started walking in my direction down the street. I noticed one of the girls trying to stall and walk slowly in order for Cee to catch up with her, while the other ran past where I was parked and went into a small, white house across the street. This was my chance to get the hell out of dodge before Cee noticed me camped out on the corner. I wanted to see what the young ho was up to, but I had to make my move before I was spotted.

After driving back to the house and parking my car in the driveway, I ran inside, stripped off my coat, and laid down in the bed as if I had been there all night. Cee walked in the house about fifteen minutes after I got settled in and began peeling off his clothes without saying a word to me.

"Where you been, Cee?" I asked, still looking at the television.

"Out," he replied dryly, while loosening the laces on his Timberland boots.

"Why didn't you answer your phone when I was calling you?"

He started to get angry and agitated because of my immediate questioning. "I left it in my car after the last time you called and hopped in the car with Will for a minute to handle some business. What's up with all the questions? Damn."

I knew he was lying, because he always got upset and frustrated whenever he had to come up with a lie for something I asked him.

"Whatever, Cee. If you would have come in the house at a decent hour, I wouldn't have to ask you anything."

"Well, if I came in when you wanted me here, you wouldn't have that damn ring on your finger. So kill it, okay, Desiree?"

Cee laid down in the bed and turned his back to me without saying another word. I decided it was worthless and chose not to continue with the argument. My mind raced with all sorts of things I wanted to say, because this fool was sure enough busted.

A few minutes later, he hopped up out of the bed, dug into his pants pocket, and retrieved his cell, which he powered off. He then plugged it into the charger and laid back down without speaking another word to me for the rest of the night.

I learned early in my day that if your man turns off his cell at night, it is always one sign that your man may be cheating. Who in the hell would be calling in the wee hours of the morning anyway? People knew when Cee came in, it was over for the night.

I laid there and blankly stared at the deep waves in the back of his head until I drifted off to sleep. I was truly fed up with his shit, but what was I going to do about it? I knew there was nothing I could say or do about it tonight besides lay here, go to sleep, and pray for a better tomorrow.

Chapter Eight

The next few days were dry and, for the most part, calm. Cee stayed gone most of the day, and I spent most of my days with his family or Shelly. I dreaded being around them because I was still weary of them for the way they kept the information about the baby from me. I kept them close only to keep him close, but I knew they were down for him in the end, not me.

One afternoon, I had Shelly pick me up from Cee's mother's house because he was trying to keep me on a short leash by taking me where he wanted me to go so he could keep a better watch over me, which I hated, because he made me feel like I was his child. He began to notice that I was getting out the house more often, so in return he would ask me to ride with him so he could later drop me off at his mother's and leave me there until he returned. That day, Shelly wanted to go to the park and hang out. So, I agreed to go along with her just so I could get away from the constant watch of his family.

Sundays at the park were like a mini fashion show and a way for people to mingle and to keep up with the who's who in Cincinnati. I didn't feel like being bothered with the lames out there that would try to hit on me, but agreed to go so I could get out and keep up with the street gossip. Not dressed at all to go to the park, I had Shelly stop by my house first, so I could change into something a little more appropriate.

When Shelly pulled up to my house, I noticed our front door was slightly ajar. This was odd, because I knew Cee didn't do sloppy shit like this. I instantly panicked and called him immediately.

"Cee, where you at?" I asked, nervous.

"Not far. Why? What's up?"

"Our fucking door is cracked open at the townhouse," I replied, both uneasy and mad that Cee was being short with me.

When he responded, he spoke with a little more bass in his voice. "What you mean? You go in there yet?"

"No, I'm sitting outside in the car with Shelly. Do you want me to check it out or wait for you?"

"Naw, don't go in there. Wait for me. I'm on my way," he said, then disconnected the call.

Shelly, being the nosy one, was eager to go in and play Inspector Gadget. She was all too anxious to go in and find out what was going on. "Girl, come on, we can go in by ourselves. Don't be scared. Somebody could have robbed y'all."

"I know, but do you think it's safe? Somebody can be in there waiting for us to come in and Cee said not to go inside."

"You know how to fight, don't you? I'll get my crowbar out my trunk and you got your pepper spray, right?" Shelly asked, getting out the car, ready to battle.

I answered reluctantly because Cee had already told me not to go in and I knew he would be heated once he found out I went against his word. "Yeah."

"Well, let's go." Shelly led the way as I slowly followed behind her.

We entered the house quietly, waiting for somebody to jump out or try and attack us. Upon entering my home, I stood frozen and in shock, unable to move past the kitchen. I immediately started crying when I realized the destruction that was done to our home. Our belongings were scattered everywhere. Papers were all over the floor. Our bar stools were all knocked over. The refrigerator was pulled out and food was all over the kitchen floor. It was total destruction. Whoever had come in here and vandalized our place was definitely looking for something.

I ran upstairs and checked our bedrooms. They were also destroyed, but nothing that I could immediately notice was missing. None of our clothing, televisions, or jewelry was missing. Everything was still there.

"Desiree, get the fuck down here!" Shelly yelled from downstairs.

I ran down the steps so fast, I almost fell over missing the last step.

Shelly stood in the middle of the kitchen, holding up various pictures. "Isn't this the bitch from the club that I whacked?"

I took the pictures from Shelly to examine. "Yeah, this the bitch. Her name is Terra," I replied, shaking my head because I was confused as to why these pictures were in my house.

Some of the pictures were of Terra by herself, two were of her and Cee, and some were with Terra and a baby boy.

"Where did you find these?" I asked confused.

"They were on the floor. Some were inside the vent over there and some were scattered with these papers," Shelly said, kicking around the papers that were on the floor. "Looks like whoever came through here was really looking for something serious. They tore open vents and shit." Shelly stared at me sadly as tears started to form in my eyes while I studied the pictures.

I completely lost it. I couldn't contain my feelings any longer. I busted out crying uncontrollably and fell to my knees. This was all too much for me to handle. I felt like I was about to have an anxiety attack and lose my mind. I was tired of pretending to be hard, acting like everything was sweet when my life was in total disarray. My house was a mess, and Cee had the audacity to hide some pictures of another female in our home.

Shelly wrapped her arms around me tightly and tried to help console my pain, but I was a furious and wounded. I wiped my face and eagerly tried to regain my composure when I heard the pounding music coming from Cee's truck outside.

"Help me get these pictures up and put them in my purse." I stood and furiously began to gather the pictures and put the vent back into place. "I don't want Cee to know I found them."

Shelly looked at me in total disbelief, but started helping me gather up all the pictures and quickly shoved them into my purse.

Another thing I learned being in this relationship was to never let a man know your every move, because they will and can use any information you have against you, which may end up backfiring on you. Men know how to flip the situation around to make you seem like the bad guy, so they can play the victim. I had to always strategically plan and prepare for the future, or lack thereof. Never let your man know the evidence that you have gathered against him. Stack your cards accordingly so you would have the winning hand in the end.

* * * *

Cee figured someone was trying to rob us, well not us, but him personally. Which meant they were looking for cash or drugs. He didn't keep anything at the house, so it was a blown mission. This was our home where we had to sleep and as he always said, "Never shit where you sleep." So, if nothing was brought in, nothing could be taken out. It didn't matter to Cee that the incident was over and nothing had been taken; he had made up his mind we had to move. I hated moving, because we had been living at our townhouse for almost two years and never had one problem until now. I really loved our house, but I also respected his mind. If he said we had to go, then we had to go.

Cee refused to stay in our home another night, so we spent the next couple of days at the Hilton downtown. He didn't join me the first night until about 4:30 a.m., because he was too busy trying to gather information about who invaded our house. It was okay with me that he was out, because I needed some time alone to gather my thoughts and figure out what I was going to do regarding our relationship.

I didn't have a clue as to what my next moves were going to be. I needed to start building a life for myself. I had become so consumed with his life that I had put mine on hold. I stopped taking classes at UC once I realized I had to be there for Cee. I had no other goals or ambitions in life except to be his wife and hopefully one day the mother to his child. I never considered pursuing a career or any other means of living if Cee and I were to ever part.

I decided to call my good high school friend, Jarvis, and ended up talking to him for almost two hours after I checked in the room and settled down. He always knew how to make me smile and was also an excellent listener. A male friend like Jarvis always came in handy whenever messed up situation occurred regarding your man.

Jarvis and I talked like we were high school lovers that couldn't stay off the phone. We would use the bathroom while the phone was still attached to our ears and all. I felt comfortable talking to him, because he allowed me to get so much that I had bottled inside off my chest. He never criticized me regarding my life with Cee. I loved Jarvis as a friend, and even though I knew he wanted more, I always made it a point to thank him for being just that, a good friend.

* * * *

The next day, Cee and I ordered room service for lunch and took a short nap together. I don't know why he left his phone on, but the entire time I was trying to get some rest the damn thing kept vibrating, distracting me. I repeatedly asked him if he wanted me to answer it, and he kept saying no and to let it ring, which pissed me off.

While he remained sleep, I monitored every number that came across the caller ID whenever it vibrated. Three times in a row, a private number showed up on the screen. The fourth time it rung. I quietly picked up the phone. I silenced it, tip-toed into the bathroom, and turned the water on so he couldn't hear me answering the call.

"Hello," I whispered.

"Hey, who is this?" The man screamed into the phone so loud that I knew Cee had heard him.

My heart pounded in my chest. "This is Desiree. Are you looking for Cee?"

"Yeah, this Joe. He wanted me to come over to y'alls house to pack up y'all stuff, but ain't nobody home," Joe said in his country accent.

"Oh, I'm sorry, Joe. He's sleep now, but I'll wake him up in a few minutes and let him know you're there," I said, trying to rush him off the phone because I heard some movement outside of the bathroom.

"Thanks, sweetie. I'll be hanging around whenever he's ready."

I peeped out the door and saw Cee standing by the bed stretching.

"Okay, Joe. Bye," I said quietly and shut off the phone.

Shit, I thought to myself, knowing I was busted. The first thing Cee went for when he woke up was his phone, so I knew he was looking for it. I was about to shit bricks when Cee started walking toward the bathroom, I quickly put his phone in the back elastic of my panties and pulled my tee shirt down as far as it could go. I flushed the toilet like I had used it, and briskly exited the bathroom as he was coming in.

"Hey, baby, you up?" I asked nervously, trying to swiftly slide by him.

"Yeah, I'm going to leave in about twenty minutes, you coming with me?" Cee asked, sitting down on the toilet.

"Yeah, I guess. I'm not going to sit around here all day. When is my car going to be ready?" I asked while taking a seat on the bed, trying to distract him from paying attention to me. I sat with my back to him and erased the last caller out of his phone so he wouldn't be able to see it had been answered.

"They said this week, but I don't know!" Cee screamed out of the bathroom, then shut the door half way.

I placed his phone back on the nightstand exactly as he had left it and was startled and almost jumped out of my skin when he flung the bathroom door open.

"Hey, baby, could you bring me my phone please?" He was sitting on the toilet with the door wide open, staring directly at me. I just knew I was busted.

"Yeah, I was just looking for an outlet so I could charge my phone. Mine is almost dead," I lied, fidgeting around, trying to find a reason to be hovering over the nightstand where his belongings were.

I accidently knocked the phone on the floor, picked it up, and took the phone in to him like it had never been touched. I needed to relax and change the mood, so I turned the water on in the shower and prepared to get in. As soon as I stepped in, tears began streaming down my face out of nowhere. I wasn't sad or anything, but I guess my guilty conscious was getting the best of me.

"You all right, Desi?" he asked while washing his hands.

"Yeah, baby, I was just washing my face. You getting in with me?" I asked, trying to divert the situation so he wouldn't keep asking me questions.

I peeked my head outside the shower curtain and noticed him taking off his clothes in the other room.

"I'm coming boo, hold up," he yelled as he picked up his vibrating phone and sent the caller to the voicemail.

"You on the phone?" I asked, trying to see who he was ignoring.

"Naw, I'm on my way in," he replied, and slid his phone into his pants pocket and walked slowly back to the bathroom.

We hadn't taken a shower together in so long that I began to wonder if he was still attracted to me. I was beginning to feel insecure, knowing that he had been intimate with another woman. Before, he would tell me all the time how beautiful and sexy I was. Now, it was only when we were dressed to go out somewhere. What use to be our daily ritual was now becoming non-existent. When Cee got into the shower, he stood and looked at me up and down like he was examining every inch of my body. I instantly caught an attitude and went into defense mode.

"What?" I snapped.

"Nothing. Damn, can't I admire my woman's beauty every now and then?" He took my face in his strong hands, began kissing me softly under the steam of the hot water, and instructed me to turn around.

Without any hesitation, I turned around, closed my eyes, and relaxed, as he started kissing me on my neck while holding my body close to his. I felt the warmth of his tongue leaving a trail of saliva down my spine, causing my legs to weaken. He came back up and gently bent me over so he could insert himself from behind. I bent over, arched my back, grabbed hold of my ankles for balance, and relaxed my body as he slowly slid himself into my pulsating flesh of wetness.

Our lovemaking was more than just the act within itself, because so much passion was involved. Today, it

71

was like he actually cared about my feelings and how he was making me feel. When he noticed I was getting tired of the position, he turned me around and pinned me up against the back of the shower. I positioned my legs around his strong back, wrapped my arms firmly around his neck, and rested my head on his shoulder inhaling his masculine aroma. I screamed out in exhilaration because of the intense pressure I was feeling while he steadily thrusted himself in and out of my body, feeding me the affection I was longing for. He managed to take me to a far-away place in my fantasy world way beyond the shower.

After our sex-capade, we got dressed and headed out. He convinced me to stay at his mom's until he got back from making some moves, which wasn't an argument nor problem after putting it on me like that in the shower. I chilled with his mom and sister, playing cards and watching television until I got tired. I eventually laid down on her sofa and drifted off to sleep while watching re-runs of Martin.

Cee picked me up from his mom's around 9:30 p.m. and rushed me out the house so we could make it to Maggiano's before they closed. On our way to the restaurant, he explained to me that he needed for me to go stay with my mom or Shelly for a while until he finished taking care of some business. This arrangement sounded too suspicious for my liking, especially with the mess I had found at the house. First, he didn't want me out of his sight, now all of a sudden he needed me to leave. I wasn't buying it.

"For what? Where are you going?" I asked, instantly getting an attitude.

"I said I have to handle something. I don't want you around to potentially become involved in anything. I can't have nobody try to hurt you on the strength of me."

"Are you serious right now, Cee?"

"Yeah. Now where do you want to go so I can set it up for you?" he asked, getting aggravated that I was questioning his authority.

"Where are you going to stay? We don't even have a place yet."

"I'm gonna chill at the other apartment and sleep at my mom's at night."

"Then why can't I stay at your mom's with you at night and chill with Shelly in the day?" I asked, becoming more apprehensive of his answers.

"Because I will just be sleeping there, and you know my little sister just came back from college this week. She will be in the other bedroom, so I'll be sleeping on the sofa."

"Cee, this is crazy. Shelly only has one bedroom, and you want me to go over to my mom's in Indiana and have to deal with her and her begging? Hell no! You know I hate it there. Why can't we just get a hotel until you finish whatever it is that you have to do?"

I could tell he was growing angrier when he started to get loud and frustrated. "Because I said so. Just take a fucking vacation or something. Damn! I don't care where you go. Just figure something out and let me know!" He huffed and screamed.

All I could do was sit back in my seat and think about what I was going to do and where could I possibly go at the last minute. I folded my arms across my chest and began to cry silently.

This fool must think I have "dummy" written across my forehead if he thinks for a second I believe him. He thinks he's slick, but we're gonna find out who is slicker, motherfucker.

Chapter Nine

Shelly and I decided to take a week's vacation in Atlanta so I could get away and cool my jets. She knew these guys who played for the Falcons that were a riot, but cool peoples, so we were bound to have fun. The guys were very nice and respectful, which is more than I can say about some of the other NFL players I knew who were strange or too arrogant for their own good. They took us to very nice restaurants and exclusive clubs that you had to be on a list to get in. We frequented various strip clubs that were also really nice. I didn't mind going strip clubs at all, because I found myself having a better time there than at the regular night clubs. Men came to pay for chicks to entertain them, so most of the time their attention wasn't on me, and I was cool with that. I was happy with what I had at home.

Saturday night, we went to this gigantic strip club and were having a blast, chilling and drinking amongst ourselves, when this handsome guy stepped to me and tried spitting game.

"I don't mean any disrespect, sweetheart, but I'd rather give you this stack of cash instead of jacking it off on any of these ladies in here. You are the finest thing up in here, and I would be very pleased if you would accept it." He stood there holding out a wad of money out for me to have like I was a cocktail waitress at the club.

I knew he was trying to impress me, but I couldn't be bought that easily, so I had to come back and hit him hard.

"Well, that is very sweet of you," I responded as sexy as I could sipping on my amaretto sour. "But you can keep your little money. I've spent that much in here already. However, a candlelight dinner might entice me a little more. How does that sound *Mr. Bankroll*? You think you can handle that, sweetheart?" I batted my eyes, flirting, like a sneaky cat and rubbed my finger down his cheek.

"Sounds like your game is a little better than mine, little lady," the guy laughed aloud. "The name's Chris Johnson. Pleased to meet you, my queen," he said, then stuffed the money back into his pocket and reached out his hand for me to shake.

Chris had the smooth-talker look, like he could sweet talk any young thing out of her panties with a blink of an eye. He stood a little over six feet tall and weighed about two hundred and thirty pounds. He had the sexy, athletic look going on, like a football player, and wore a fitted, cream tee that made his sexy muscles bulge out of his shirt. What I liked most about his appearance was his slanted, almond eyes complimented by beautiful long, thick, dark eyelashes. When he stuck his hand out, I noticed that his nails were freshly manicured, which was a good touch. I looked down to check out his shoe game, which was also on point. He wore a pair of cream and gray Prada sneakers that matched the stitching in his pants. Just his style alone had me going.

"The name's Desiree, and it's my pleasure," I said, trying not to show any interest on my face. "So what time should I be ready, Mr. Johnson."

"Let's say 9 a.m., 3 p.m., and 8:30 p.m. Breakfast, lunch, and dinner," Chris replied, never taking his eyes off of me.

"You have yourself a triple date then. Don't bite off more than you can handle now," I responded, flirtatiously accepting Chris's offer.

He retrieved a business card out of a silver card case and handed it to me, with instructions to call him right away so he could save my number in his phone. I played it cool and didn't call for about an hour, just to see if he tried running that same game on anyone else, and to see how sharp his memory was.

He didn't answer his phone when I called, and I wasn't about to call him again or blow him up just because he looked good. I hung up the phone without leaving a message to see how he would respond when he called back. The man was on point when he returned my call about fifteen minutes later. I answered my phone on the last ring so it wouldn't come off like I was eager or anticipating his call. Before I could get out a complete hello, he cut me off.

"So how was your night, Desiree?" he asked, sounding all sexy with his deep voice. I was astonished because he remembered my name, the times of our dates, and even complimented me on my attire. I didn't know if it was because I was calling from another area code or what that gave him the clues who I was, but I was flattered and surprisingly eager to take on my new adventure.

Chris occupied the rest of my vacation, and I was happy to spend the rest of it with someone who appreciated me and my time. I looked forward to spending more and more time with Chris in the near future. Cee had only called me about six times the entire time I was in Atlanta, and our conversations were bland and short. I didn't bother him much and he wasn't bothering me. I enjoyed my time being pampered by Chris. He wined and dined me, and massaged and caressed my body in a way that I hadn't felt in a long time. I didn't realize another man could touch my body and make me feel the way I did when I was with him.

"Do you have to go so soon?" Chris asked, poking out his bottom lip while feeding me plump red grapes, as I relaxed in his king-sized bed.

"Yes, I'm sorry. I'm afraid I do." I regretted those words as they left my mouth. "I have to. My mom is looking forward to me coming to see her for at least one day."

"How about if I fly you up to see your mom next week?"

"Then, who will ride back to Cincinnati with Shelly? I can't have her drive up there all by herself."

"She can stay, too. I just want you here a little longer. She can stay in my guest room. Or I can fly her back when she's ready to go. Just ask her," Chris begged.

"All right, I'll call her. She might be game since we won't have to drive back home."

I grabbed my cell out of my purse and called Shelly, who was still with her friend, Terrance, scoring touchdowns.

"What up, Shell?"

"Shit, chilling with my boo...about to pack it up. You enjoying yourself, girl?"

"You know it. I think I'm enjoying myself a little too much, 'cause I don't want to leave."

"Well, you know I have to have this rental back, and I have to go to work on Wednesday," Shelly said while giggling, but obviously not at me.

"How about you turn the rental in here at this airport and fly back Tuesday evening?"

"What are you talking about, girl?" Shelly asked and busted out laughing. "Stop, will ya. I'm on the phone, T," Shelly said to Terrance. "I'm sorry, girl. This fool plays too much. Now what was you saying?"

I got to the point, because obviously Terrance was trying to get her attention. "I want you to stay down here with me for a couple more days. I'm not ready to leave yet."

"Damn, the dick is that good huh? Bitch don't even want to go home," she busted out laughing, then continued. "What do you think Cee is going to say?"

"I really don't really care. He wanted me to leave, so I left. And I'm having a wonderful time. You can only push a girl so far until she leaves for good and doesn't want to come back, ya know?"

"Okay, Maya Angelou. I'm game. I can only stay until Tuesday. No ifs, ands, or your butt. You're crazy. You know that, Ree?"

"I don't care. Crazy is as crazy does. I'm having a wonderful time and I deserve it. I'm going to take advantage of every moment while I'm here until I have to return to my so called life. You know all fairy tales have to end one day, my princess." I laughed, but was dead serious, because I meant every word I had said.

"I'll have Terrance drop me off. See you in a minute. I haven't heard you laugh like that in forever, sis. I'm glad you're finally happy again."

"Me too, sis. See ya later!"

I didn't realize my happiness was actually that obvious. I was happy, and it was sad because it didn't take much to make me feel good. All a girl needed was a little attention and love every once in a while to keep her content. I could easily be happy with Cee if he only treated me like he really loved me instead of saying that he did and, in return, doing some bullshit. Yes, he said and promised me a lot, and showered me with material things, yet I was still waiting and yearning for those words to one day turn into actions. I couldn't understand how he didn't notice that I was hurting and wanting him to tend to my feelings and emotions that were being neglected. If he only showed me a portion of the attention he gave the streets, everything would be perfect.

Men don't really understand that work, whether nine to five or in the streets, can ruin a relationship if they can't manage to equally divide work time and quality time, because time spent does matter. In my case, our difference in views was causing a detrimental distance between me and the man I loved. Here I was with a new man and not even feeling guilty, because he was providing me with the attention that I was craving. I believe that Cee was too comfortable with our relationship and felt like I should just roll with it because I was his girl, but he was sadly mistaken.

Chapter Ten

My fairy tale with Chris ended too soon and I was faced with my real life before I knew it. I enjoyed my time so much with Chris that I actually entertained the thought of leaving Cee for him. I knew I wasn't going to up and leave Cee just because I found something that appeared to be more suitable, but I allowed myself to toy with the idea a little. Chris owned his own company and had a good career. The most important part was that he made me feel appreciated, like a man should, and spent quality time with me, which I needed. I appreciated that, and most importantly, I appreciated him. Shelly picked me up from the airport and we went over my story as if I had been in Indiana the entire time. Cee never called and asked where I was, if I needed anything, or even checked on me to see if I was okay. He just went through the motions. Random calls and texts to say what's up were the extent of it. He never made it a point to include me in things that went on his life, so I didn't feel it was necessary for me to volunteer any of my personal business about what went on during my trip to him.

"Cee, where are you, and where am I supposed to go? I'm home," I said with an attitude as soon as I heard his voice.

"Go to my mom's. I'll pick you up from there. I'm looking at this condo now," he replied, then ended the call without so much as a 'Hey, baby, how you doing?' or 'How was the trip?' Nothing. Just cut and dry.

Although I was against the idea, I told Shelly to drop me off at Ms. Marie's house to avoid an argument. I was tired from the plane ride anyway. So, as soon as I got in, I decided to take a nap and wait for Cee to come to the house. The nap would be a good refresher to help me deal with Cee's attitude before he came to pick me up. I preferred a strong alcoholic beverage, but a nap would have to suffice.

I woke up around 8:30 p.m. and noticed two missed calls from Chris, but none from Cee. I asked his sister, Alicia, and his mom if they had heard from him, and they both said no. I called his phone and got the voicemail. I called again, but still no answer. As soon as I hung up, I got a call from a restricted number. I normally didn't answer restricted callers, but I figured I'd better because it could be Cee.

I immediately answered with an attitude. "Who is this?"

Cee spoke out of breath, as if he had been running a marathon. "Baby, this is me. Somebody just ran me off the fucking road. I need you to come get me. I'm at the McDonald's and Shell gas station off Mitchell."

My heart started beating uncontrollably as tears began to well up in the ducts of my eyes. "What you mean, baby? What happened?"

"Just get here. I'll fill you in later. Grab my thing from underneath the sofa and hurry up. I don't know what the fuck is going on. My fucking car is totaled," he yelled, breathing hard, then slammed the phone.

I ran into the living room, grabbed Cee's gun from underneath the sofa, snatched Marie's spare keys to the Range off the coffee table, and ran out the house. My nerves were all over the place. He had me beyond nervous and shaky as hell. All I could do was pray that he was okay and safe.

* * * *

Damn, this is fucked up, Cee thought to himself while searching in his pockets for more change so he could make another call. His mind was racing a million miles a minute trying to figure out what had just happened. He never had any run-ins like this before, because he kept it cool with everyone in the city. Everyone respected him around the hood because of all the good deeds he did within the community, and how he never associated himself with any petty drama or bullshit when it came to his business.

Cee wasn't the type of guy who caused drama or even wanted to be involved in it. He was all about making money and helping those who were trying to do the right things to help themselves. He went as far as schooling his guys about spending time with their families, and made sure every one of his workers that had children set up an account and put away at least one hundred dollars a week for their kid's education and for life insurance.

He hadn't a clue who would try to fuck with him, because even though he had a good heart, he wasn't soft by far. A couple niggas in the past got their issue trying to size him up, and he had no problem serving them the beef that they ordered. Cee handled his business very professionally and left the dirty work up to his right-hand man Will or Will's trigger happy crew.

He had to get up with Will and quick, so he could keep his ear to the streets and find out what was going on. He knew it probably had to be some young stick-up kids who didn't know who they were messing with, so he didn't make the call to Will urgent. He picked up the receiver and inserted his last quarter to make his final call. He hated that he even had to call this number and deliver bad news, because he couldn't deal with her nagging every time she didn't get her way.

"What's up, Terra?" Cee said, sounding annoyed so Terra would get the hint.

"Waiting on you. Where you at?"

"Look, something came up and I'm not going to be able to make it. We'll have to reschedule for another day."

"What the fuck you mean? I told you that today was the only day I was off, and you said we were going to have family time this week, Cee," Terra cried, putting an emphasis on 'you' as she spoke. "I think you doing this on purpose. I've done everything you asked and been cool, and now you going to come at me with this?"

He cut her off before she could finish. "I said something came up. Damn!" Cee yelled. "I don't have time for this Terra. I'll call you tomorrow!"

"Well, where you at, and why aren't you calling me from your phone? You on some sneaky shit, Cee, and I ain't feeling it," Terra continued.

Cee's patience was wearing thin. "Bye, Terra," he huffed.

"No, but wait. What about Darius?" Terra added quickly before Cee prepared to hang up on her.

His patience was becoming non-existent. He couldn't handle her whining ass or Desiree's million questions he knew she would ask after showing up. Therefore, he had to end the call.

"I said bye, Terra. Damn!" he yelled, then slammed down the phone's receiver, leaving a weeping Terra still on the line.

* * * *

When I pulled up to the McDonald's and didn't see Cee, I instantly got worried. I parked the truck as if I was getting some gas and sat there anxiously waiting for him to appear from some ducked off spot. After about three minutes, I saw him walking out of the McDonald's, eating some fries like nothing happened.

He opened the driver's side door and instructed me to move over to the passenger's seat. "I got to make a stop real quick," Cee said calmly.

"What the fuck is up?" I screamed. "You rushed me out here like you were in danger, and you walk out here eating French fries like nothing happened."

"Man, it's cool, baby." Cee leaned over and gave me a quick peck on the lips before he continued. "I don't know what was going on. I was going to drop off this package and pick up my bread from Al after I got finished with what I was doing earlier. That's when I noticed some niggas following me. So, I made a detour to try and spin them, but they stayed on my tail. They followed me from Covington all the way to Mitchell and wasn't letting up. The niggas got all up on my ass and started flashing their high beams and shit. Then, out of the blue, the niggas started ramming my car from the back. I tried to speed up and lose them, but they came on the side of me and ran my fucking car into the ditch. Fucked my Benz all up! I was riding dirty, so I couldn't call the cops, and I didn't want them to be all up in my business if one rolled up being nosy. So, I just left the car there and came here to call you," he explained, still stuffing fries into his mouth as he spoke.

I was confused because this didn't make any sense. Cee never had problems before to this extent, and now he was just sitting there all nonchalant.

"Where is your cell?" I asked suspiciously.

"Shit, I don't know. I couldn't find it. I wasn't really trying to look for it, either. I had to get away from there to stash my pack before the boys rode by," he said, licking the salt off of his fingers.

We got back on the highway and stopped off by some bushes so Cee could retrieve the package that he stashed in case the police had come to investigate the accident. After he picked up his bag, we made a quick stop downtown by his boy Al's apartment building so he could pick up his money. My baby was smart and usually stayed on his game, but this was getting a little crazy and I wasn't trying to deal with hood drama anymore. I didn't have a clue if the guys were still on his trail, watching him, or what. I just wanted us to get away permanently so he didn't get hurt.

"You didn't tell my mom anything, did you?" Cee asked as he got back in the car, checking inside the large, blue duffle bag to make sure all of his cash was there.

"No, I just grabbed her spare keys off the table and left. Why don't I have keys to the Range, Cee? I got the keys to the Benz, so what's the difference?" I asked, changing the subject.

"What you need them for?" He asked, cutting his eyes at me.

"In case shit like this were to happen, or if you needed me for anything and I don't have my car."

Cee didn't answer. Instead, he just gave me a stank-ass look.

"I'm just saying, you never know what can happen, *obviously*. I need to know I can be there for you if you need me."

"If I ever need you, you'll have a way. Trust me. Let's leave this alone, okay?"

"Whatever. Trust you? Yeah, okay," I rolled my eyes and leaned back in my seat as he pulled off, ignoring my last comment.

After about a half hour drive, he tapped me on the shoulder and woke me up as he pulled into a garage of an unfamiliar apartment complex.

"Where are we?" I asked, still half asleep.

"This is the new spot I was telling you about," he said with a grin on his face.

"Thanks for letting me know. So you mean to tell me we live here now?" I asked, sarcastically.

"It's a surprise. Come on," Cee said and hopped out the truck, grabbing his duffle bag from the back seat.

I couldn't believe how his demeanor flipped flopped just like that, like he was bipolar or something. Something about him wasn't right lately. I'm not sure if it was the baby drama or this mess about someone running him off the road, but I was going to have to find out. Earlier, he was all hysterical and paranoid, and now a couple of hours later, he's overjoyed with surprises. I couldn't keep up with him and all his various personalities.

As I walked up the steps from the garage, I noticed the apartment was already furnished, and there was no second floor to the unit like we had at the townhouse. I guess the main level was the upstairs because the garage was underneath.

"Go on ahead and look around. Tell me what you think," Cee instructed as he took a seat at the dining room table and started counting his money.

I kicked off my Nikes at the entrance to the living room and admired the thickness of the carpet as my feet sunk into the plush, soft fibers. I was hesitant to even look around at first, because this wasn't like Cee to make decisions without me. I slowly browsed the unfamiliar apartment that I was now supposed to call my new home. I was kind of upset because I didn't have the luxury of picking out the furniture or accessories; it was already decorated for us. Everything was nicely arranged, so I didn't bother complaining and have him think I was ungrateful.

"Who decorated?" I screamed from the bathroom in the hallway as I switched the light on and admired the dark wood cabinets.

"The decorator I guess. It was a model home."

I walked in the first room and could tell it was designed to be a guestroom. It was furnished with a queen-sized, metal-framed bed and matching furniture. A gold and burgundy, plush Jacquard comforter set draped over the bed with matching accent pillows. Whoever slept in there would be sleeping very comfortably. Various pictures and gold accessories adorned the dark tan walls that were trimmed in a diamond-patterned wallpaper, which added a nice touch. A nice-sized plasma television was mounted to the wall over the mantle of the small electric fireplace. A large plant sat in the corner by the window, which gave the room an open, earthy feel.

After making my way to the very back of the apartment, I opened two French doors to what had to be the master bedroom. The room was enormous! The cherry hardwood floors were sparkling like they had been freshly waxed that same day. I slid across the floor in my socks, pretending like a rock star with a guitar and instantly fell in love. I could tell why he picked this condo. The master bedroom could sell itself! The bedroom was the size of the entire front of the house, which was also large. It reminded me of a circular family room rather than a bedroom.

In the center of my new bedroom was a huge wooden canopy bed with large twisted posts. The comforter was beige suede with a rope-like, dark brown trim. A ton of pillows were neatly positioned around the headboard and base of the bed, which made me want to hop in and roll around like a kid.

"Hey, baby, is the bed in our room new or was it included in the model?" I asked.

"Yeah, it's new. I got it delivered today. I picked it out while you were out of town," he screamed.

I walked around the huge room and touched everything, marveling at the quality and style of the pieces that were selected. A low, dark-brown, microfiber loveseat was positioned at the foot of our bed, which added to the coziness of the room. I looked up and noticed a projector mounted to the ceiling, directed toward the large white space on the wall over a small electric fireplace, just like the one in the spare bedroom. The fireplace was accented with various pieces of African art and vases with sticks and bamboo that sat on each side. I went over to the large, circular bay window and admired the view of the sparkling lake from our bedroom. With my fingertips, I rubbed the leaves of the tropical-looking plants that were surrounding the window to see if they were artificial, but they were real! I was in love with my new place, and knew there would be amazing things to come in this room.

While gazing out the window and taking in the serenity of the view, my thoughts were suddenly interrupted when I heard a noise coming from inside the closet door.

"Baby, there's a rumbling noise coming from the bedroom closet. Get in here!" I screamed.

I stood frozen by the window, listening to what seemed to be a constant shuffling noise coming from behind the closet door. And after what had happened earlier, my nerves were anything but calm. I tapped on the door to see if it was just a mouse or something, 'cause if so, we definitely weren't staying here...no matter how much I loved the place. The noise stopped for a minute, and I began to wonder why he hadn't come running in yet to check it out.

After mustering up enough courage to open the large door, I instantly jumped back, becoming startled at first by the sight before me. All I could do was cover my mouth and cry. Cee had bought me a little puppy, and it was the kind I had always wanted, a black and brown teacup yorkie. I was ecstatic because it was so cute. It had a little red bow around its neck and everything. When I picked it up, I noticed poop in the corner of the large his and hers walk-in closet.

"How long have you been in there, little fella?" I cooed to the dog, talking to it like a baby. "Thank you so much, Cee. It is too cute," I said, running to the kitchen with the dog cradled in my arms.

Cee met me in the hallway and out of the blue, started passionately kissing me, while the dog rested on my shoulder.

"Happy Birthday, baby," he said, smiling. "You like him?"

"Of course, I like him, but my birthday is not until Tuesday."

"I know. You weren't supposed to get him until then. I was supposed to stop by here before I picked you up and take the dog over to Will's until that bullshit happened. What you want to name him?"

"I don't know. It's a boy, right?

"Yeah." Cee roughly rubbed the small dog's head with his large hand.

"How about Gizmo. What you think, baby?"

"Hey, little fella, you like the name Gizmo?" he asked, all up in the dog's face.

The little dog actually barked. I'm not sure if it was because Cee was too close to his face or because he actually liked the name. Either way, it was official. Gizmo would be his name.

I know this may sound dumb to some, but I felt like Cee and I were really starting to come together again. Buying this dog for me meant more than a nice gesture or birthday present. He knew I was getting lonely and needed some companionship when he wasn't around, so Gizmo was the perfect makeup gift. I felt like I actually had a little family now with me, Cee, and our new addition, Gizmo.

Chapter Eleven

Spring was rapidly approaching. So, that meant Cee was gone most of the day, working in the streets and out handling his business. At times, it seemed like I only saw him for about twenty hours out of the week. It may be a slight exaggeration, but that's how I felt. He was out doing what he did best and also training for the spring basketball tournaments that were coming up. His boys knew his time in the streets would be drastically cut when the basketball season started, so they were working him like crazy.

Cee sponsored a team called The Pit, which was made up of guys of all ages from our hood. It was a good idea to get guys from around the city to be a part of something positive instead of shooting up and fighting each other all the time. Cee's team always came out on top every season and he planned to keep it that way. People from all over made bets on these games, and Cee always made sure he had his dibs in with his favorite teams besides his own. He always managed to come home with lots of money to spare, so I never complained.

His main concern lately was on the streets and coaching his team; so the more he was away, the more time I spent conversing with Chris. We remained cool ever since I left Atlanta and talked here and there, about three times a week. The further Cee distanced himself from me, the closer I got to Chris. I secretly planned a weekend trip to go see Chris before the first basketball games started and while Cee's focus was on everything else besides me.

* * * *

"Hey, baby, it's me," I said into the phone sweetly.

Cee yelled something to his team before replying. "Hey, what's up? You getting ready to go to your mom's?" he asked, out of breath.

"Yeah, I'll be leaving about six tonight. I cleaned up, so don't mess up the house please. And I left your dinner in the fridge. I'll be back before Sunday's game. What time does it start again?"

"Three o'clock, so you better be there, Desi. This is the opening game and we are having a party afterwards. You need any money?"

"No, I'm straight. I don't plan on doing any shopping or anything while I'm there. Me and my family are just going to chill. I'll see you Sunday. I'll call you when I get there. Love you."

"I love you, too. Make sure you feed Gizmo, because I don't know when I'm going to be in. My sister will be over later, but I don't know what time. Be good and be safe."

"All right, baby. Bye," I ended the call and zipped up the last of my luggage.

I'm glad he reminded me that Alicia was coming over to the house, because I completely forgot. She was bringing some guy over that she had recently met, because she knew Marie wasn't with having strange men in her house.

I later found out that Cee had Alicia put our condo in her name so it couldn't be traced after the shit that happened at our townhouse. I wasn't sure if Cee didn't trust me or what, but I wasn't feeling the fact that I was living under the roof of a home that wasn't technically mine. I left fifty dollars and a note on the table for Alicia so she could pick up some food for Gizmo because I was already running behind and didn't want to miss my flight.

After gathering my bags, I rushed out the house and headed to CVG Airport.

* * * *

Alicia couldn't wait to hook up with her new boo again. They had become very close since the last time they hung out. She was hoping he would get tired of creeping around at other people's houses and ask her to move in with him. She was really feeling him and she could tell he was equally feeling her. He talked a little too much for her taste, but she dealt with it because he was telling her everything she wanted to hear.

Cee let her borrow his new Benz for the day so she could get back and forth from the house, so she was overly ecstatic. She made it a point to take the street route to Cee's house so she could be seen and stunt in the streets in her brother's new car. She even offered to pick her date up so he could get a hint of her style, but he politely declined and insisted on driving his own car. Her boo wasn't the flashy type. He had no idea what he was getting himself into dealing with her, because she was sure enough just like her brother and appreciated the finer things in life and got whatever she wanted.

Alicia let herself in the condo with her spare key and noticed the note Desiree had left her on the coffee table. She picked it up, sighed with aggravation, and then dialed her new friend.

"Hey, J, this is Alicia. I'm at my brother's now. Do you mind picking up some dog food? This tramp didn't even have the decency to feed her own dog before she left. Thanks. See you when you get here, boo."

Chapter Twelve

The two nights I spent with Chris just wasn't enough. Once again, I didn't want to leave. He and I had a wonderful time together, and he catered to me and made me feel special all over again. He was like my occasional drug and I was in desperate need of a fix. We hung out with some of his friends and he took me to a prestigious art gallery, which was lovely. What tripped me out was that he didn't pressure me for sex at all, and I appreciated it because he wore me out with all the activities we were involved in during the day.

Over all, we had sex about three times while I was there, and he kind of upset me the last time when he kept insisting that we have anal sex, which I didn't get down with. Chris was a freak. He would try to finger me in the ass and all, which caused me to think he might have been down with the *opposite team*. He ate my ass and everything, which was new to me 'cause Cee didn't do anything like that. I couldn't front, though; he had me turned out. I couldn't help but to think about it the entire plane ride home.

I dreaded coming home that Sunday morning, but was excited to see all of Cee's hard work pay off with his team. I drove straight to the house from the airport so I could unpack, take a hot shower to remove any lingering male scent from me, and change my clothes for the game. I slid on my Victoria's Secret jogging suit and Nikes, and headed downtown to watch the game. I got there about 4:15 p.m., and surprisingly, it was packed already. The Pit was last to play, so I was okay on time. They were the only team I cared to see anyway.

After walking around and exchanging greetings with the people I knew from the hood, I asked one of Cee's boys where he was. One of the excited kids that were running around playing tag said he was over by the grill the last time he had seen him. I should have just looked for the group of females that swarmed like lions around a fresh piece of meat. Wherever Cee was, there was always a definite chance that at least a dozen females weren't too far away. I walked over by the grill that was still smoking with every meat you could imagine cooking, deliciously smelling up the entire park. I was glad to see, once again, the success of these games that were perfect for black people to get together with no drama involved and have a good old time.

I walked through the crowd of people and came to a sudden halt. I don't think I can fully explain the excruciating pain and hurt I felt in my chest, stomach, and heart when I saw Cee standing casually on the wall with his arm wrapped around Terra's neck. Here was my man all hugged up with this bitch in public, all cheese-faced, like I wasn't in the picture. To be honest, all I could do was stand there frozen and think of what to do, because all of my body functions had completely shut down. Cee didn't notice me until Will tapped his arm and pointed in my direction. As soon as his eyes met mine, I immediately regained my composure and stormed over, fuming! I placed my hands on my hips to restrain myself from punching him in the face in front of all these people and stood waiting for an explanation.

"Hey, Desiree. How was your trip?" Shockingly, he didn't react like I expected him to. Instead, he just stood there smiling, with his arm still wrapped around Terra like his girl wasn't standing directly in front of him embarrassed and hurting.

"What the hell do you mean how was my trip? What the fuck are you doing out here with your arm wrapped all around this bitch's neck?" I asked fuming between clenched teeth.

He looked at me with an evil grin on his face. "Desiree, this is Terra. Terra, this is Desiree."

"I don't give a flying fuck who she is," I yelled, pushing his arm from around her.

"How was ATL? You have fun?" Cee asked, as he began to walk away from the crowd.

"How would I know how Atlanta was when I was in Indiana, Cee?"

He spoke nonchalantly, walking away as I trailed behind him. "No, you weren't."

"Yes the fuck I was. What's wrong with you?" I asked, and snatched his arm from behind so he would stop walking and talk to me.

"Look, Desi, I got a game to coach. You sticking around to cheer us on or what?"

"Are you serious right now? Yeah, you must be crazy to think I would be out here cheering like an idiot and you was just posted up with that bitch, embarrassing me after all we've been through with her."

"Naw, baby, you embarrassed yourself when you decided to go see...ummm, what's his name? Chris? My team's up, baby I got to go. Enjoy yourself," he said with a smirk. To add insult to injury, he tilted my mouth closed from my chin with his finger, and planted a swift peck on my cheek.

Cee jogged over to where his team was gathering and left me standing there looking stuck on stupid. I felt like the entire park was staring at me pointing, laughing, and whispering while I was being dissed by my own man in public.

All I could do was stand there with my eyes filled with tears and act like he hadn't fazed me. He had really done it this time...out here on public display with that bitch. I didn't care where I was or who I was with. Nobody played me like that!

I stormed over to my car, leaned over the steering wheel, and furiously busted out crying. All I could do was sit there and let it all out. I couldn't go back out there and act a fool, because I didn't want other people, or Terra for that matter, to see that I was hurt. I had to get the hell away from there and fast. I started the car, slammed on the gas, and sped away. Sitting at a red light, I fidgeted around the middle console for the saddest CD to listen to. I was totally depressed and fed up and needed to be able to vibe with someone that felt what I was feeling. I inserted the Mary J. Blige, Share My World CD and scrolled to play *Not Gonna Cry*, which only made me more depressed. Still, I could relate to what she was going through.

I tried calling Jarvis twice, but got his voicemail both times. I didn't see him outside, so I knew he wasn't at the game. Next, I called Shelly and told her to meet me in our old hood because I couldn't get a hold of Jarvis. I needed him bad at this moment, but really, I was in need of any kind of distraction to ease the pain I was experiencing.

During the entire ride to the hood, I sobbed like a baby, listening to *Not Gonna Cry* over and over. Although I was not going through the same things Mary was, I could definitely feel her pain.

I met Shelly at the hood bar and started tossing back shots like an alcoholic. Drinking and being around Shelly and the people from my old neighborhood made me feel a lot better. Guys that I hadn't seen in years continuously bought Shelly and me drinks, which we politely accepted.

After finally getting a hold of Jarvis, he told me he would pick me up from the bar in about an hour after he got finished doing whatever he was doing.

After about five rounds of various shots, I went from sobbing to Mary's *Not Gonna Cry*, to getting turned up to Trina's *Here We Go*, that Shelly requested, of course. I was enjoying myself a little too much, dancing and singing to all the throwbacks that the DJ played, but it was fun and relaxing to let loose for a change and get the drama from earlier off of my brain.

Shelly and I made a toast that we were going to go over to Terra's house like some true killas, drag her outside, and beat the living shit out of her, which really got me hyped. That is, until Jarvis showed up a half an hour early, stuck a pin in our plan, and deflated it, causing my party to come to a drunken end.

* * * *

Jarvis was always there for me whenever I needed him, just like a trusted knight from the fairy tales. Luckily, he rescued me from the club before Shelly and I decided to leave there drunk and possibly beat Terra to a pulp. He was very pleasant and patient the entire ride as he drove to drop Shelly off at her apartment. He remained silent while Shelly and I constantly ranted about how fucked up Cee was and how Terra had to get it. Jarvis didn't entertain drama, so I was thankful that he let me vent and talk shit freely with my girl.

After he dropped Shelly off, he stopped at a local gas station and bought me two bottled waters to help me sober up so I could tell him what was really bothering me. I knew I could always depend on Jarvis whenever I needed to get whatever frustrations I had pent up inside out in the open. He was always there when I needed a male friend to confide in, whenever Cee did something to hurt me, or whenever I was feeling lonely.

He never pressured me for sex over the years we had been cool, even though I knew he wanted to do it

104

again. We had sex one time, on his eighteenth birthday. The experience wasn't bad, but we never tried anything else after that because I never had a sexual attraction to Jarvis. I looked at him like a brother, not a lover. He knew of Cee through me, but I don't think he ever had a clue who Cee actually was. After that charade at the game and still intoxicated from the liquor, I was ready to fuck the shit out of Jarvis just because. I knew Jarvis wouldn't dare turn me away, because I always came first in his eyes.

He drove to the Hyatt Regency downtown and checked us in while I waited in the car for him to tell me which room to come to. I needed time to be alone for a minute just in case Cee decided to call and apologize. I was eager to press the button to send him straight to voicemail just to let him know I was busy for the night. He needed a taste of his own medicine, so he could feel how I was feeling and, in turn, be mad and jealous. Jarvis and I couldn't be seen checking into a hotel together anyway, because you never knew who was employed where, and I didn't want to take any chances, even if Cee had messed up again.

When we entered the room, Jarvis told me to relax and drink the water he had bought for me to sober up while he filled the Jacuzzi tub with hot water and hotel brand bubbles. After I submerged myself into the steaming tub, he massaged my legs and feet with some peppermint smelling lotion that came with the room. Whenever I cried, Jarvis wiped my tears, and whenever I ached, he rubbed my body. I communicated every feeling and emotion I was going through at that moment while I laid back in the tub, relaxed by his touch. Thankfully, he listened attentively and didn't judge me, my emotions, or feelings like a true friend. During my rant, I noticed how he would often try to turn the conversation around and focus it on the relationship he and I shared. He expressed how much he still cared for me even though I was with another man, how he would never hurt me, and promised to always keep me happy, but all I wanted to do was talk about Cee.

Jarvis would constantly compliment me by telling me how beautiful I was and how I deserved better. I knew he meant I deserved better by being in a relationship with him, but I would be taking a drastic loss if I left Cee for Jarvis. When it came down to the bedroom game, though, Jarvis was on point the first and last time we were intimate. He knew how to put it down and what it meant to please a woman.

Once I started feeling lightheaded, I got out of the tub and wrapped my dripping body in the large hotel bathrobe. I joined Jarvis in the bed as he sat on the edge smoking a blunt and drinking some leftover Grey Goose he had brought in with him while watching ESPN. I laughed to myself, figuring he needed to have a drink also to be able to deal with all my drama. I asked him if I could take a couple puffs of the weed he was smoking, just to see if it would really relax me like people said it would. Tonight, I wanted to go all out and I wasn't holding back any feelings or desires. I wanted to feel free and completely relaxed for what was about to occur.

I positioned myself behind him, wrapped my legs around his waist, and rested my head on his shoulder. I guess I was still feeling the alcohol from earlier or the weed had started to kick in, because as I laid on his shoulder, I nuzzled my face into the side of his neck and became instantly aroused by inhaling his sweet masculine sent. I began trailing my manicured nails up and down the skin of his muscular arms and touching and caressing his body more seductively than I had ever done before. Jarvis was always so gentle and careful whenever he touched me, like I was a fragile piece of art that he was afraid to damage. I nibbled on the bottom of his earlobe, causing him to slightly shiver, and softly whispered in his ear for him to turn around and look at me. After putting out his blunt in the ashtray, he twisted his body around to face me. I took his smooth baby face in my hands and started kissing him passionately like we were featuring in our very own love story. I was an aggressive female by nature and I liked for my men to be even more aggressive and take control sometimes in lovemaking, so I needed Jarvis to step it up.

He gently laid me down on the bed and untied the knot to the hotel bathrobe that I had draped over me, all while staring into my lazy, squinted eyes. He squeezed the nipple of my breast between two of his fingers in a scissor-like motion, which drove me instantly wild. The way he was looking at me was making me uneasy, and I started feeling self-conscious for some reason. I knew I was a nice sight to look at, but being with him like this made me feel weird.

Pushing my feelings to the side, I pulled his polo shirt off and swiftly started planting miniature kisses all over his chest. I pushed him down forcefully on the bed, so I could be on top of him and could take control to show him how I wanted it. He raised his hips after I unbuttoned his jeans so I could ease his pants down over his waist. I gently traced my finger up his bare leg slowly making my way up to his chest. With the tip of my tongue, I traced tiny circles around his nipples, gently biting and tugging on each one until they hardened with affection. I moved south, leaving a wet trail down to his navel then kissed and licked each muscle around his firm, sculpted stomach. Noticing his growing erection, I wrapped my hand around his large, thick penis and began skillfully massaging in a precise up and down motion, which caused him to moan out in sweet pleasure. The veins in his huge shaft began bulging and pulsating with every stroke.

Gradually, I took the head of his swollen penis into my mouth, sucking it rhythmically like I was indulging a melting popsicle. I licked, kissed, sucked, and used my lips to play with the head of his penis, teasing him and making him yearn and cry out for more. Once coated in saliva, in one smooth motion, I deep throated his entire penis like a porn star, trailing wetness all the way down to his scrotum. I gave him the head of his life. While my lips were still fixated around his large penis, he rotated my body around to the sixty-nine position so he could return the favor like a true gentleman.

In between rough sex, shots of Goose, and wrestling around like school kids, we ended up having sex like three times that night. Jarvis left the hotel around six the next morning. He left me sore as hell, but I was relaxed, stress-free, and damn sure satisfied.

Chapter Thirteen

I checked out of the hotel a little after 11:30 that morning and took a cab back to the discomforts of my broken home. The entire ride home, I felt guilty because lately I had been masking my pain with liquor and sex, and that wasn't a good look for me or my man. When I got in, Gizmo started barking like crazy, which immediately alerted Cee that I was just now coming home from yesterday.

I threw my purse on the loveseat and went into the bathroom to let my presence be known to Cee. I didn't want to make it seem like I was hiding or ashamed of my actions, so I boldly walked into the bathroom and sat on the toilet. He was in the shower rapping some 50 Cent song, never looking my way or acknowledging my presence. The sound of his voice at that moment made my soul cringe in disgust. I finished using the bathroom and intentionally flushed the toilet, hoping his water would get cold.

When he got out the shower, he came into our room and looked at me with a blank stare while drying off his body. I sat on the edge of our bed with my face buried in my hands and thought about what I was going to do with my life. I had been involved with two different

110

men, who both put forth a substantial amount of energy to keep me happy, and here I sat depressed, dealing with a man all because he kept me financially secure. Feeling half way embarrassed and guilty, I kept my face down in my lap, not wanting my eyes to meet his burning stare. I couldn't manage seeing his face at this moment, because I wasn't sure if my face would reveal my true feelings.

Cee stood directly in front of me and continued to dry off without saying a word, like I wasn't even sitting there.

When he finished with his towel, he threw it on the bed next to me. "You got that shit out your system, Desiree?" He asked dryly.

"What the fuck do you mean by that?" I responded, as my nose flared out in anger and slowly raised my head to look at him.

"Whoever you fucked last night that kept you out until now. You happy? That's what you wanted, right?"

"What are you talking about? I haven't been with anybody! I lied, feeling guilty, staring at his perfectly cut body as he rubbed lotion on his arms.

"Take your clothes off."

"What?" I asked, confused, not knowing if he was serious or not.

"I said take that shit off! Here, I'll help you since you don't seem to understand," he said as he roughly began yanking my clothes off.

"Stop!" I yelled, feeling like I was about to cry. "What's wrong with you? I'm not on this right now, Cee," I cried, struggling to get him to stop.

He kept pulling and tugging on my clothes like a mad man until he had me down to my panties and bra, which he also ripped off after examining my body with his piercing eyes. He roughly pushed me back on the bed, laid on top of me, grabbed my face with his large hand, and tried tongue kissing me. I was so upset that I didn't want my lips to even come close to his. I thought my neck was going to snap as I turned my head from side to side so he would stop. I was so utterly disgusted by his constant groping and thick saliva that I felt like I was going to vomit.

He pushed my head into the bed pinning me down by my neck and moved his body lower and roughly started sucking on my breast, one and then the other. The sharpness from his bite hurt like hell. It felt like he was intentionally trying to induce pain on me, I was beyond uncomfortable and scared of this beast of a man. He was behaving savagely and it frightened me. I was in total discomfort and tried my hardest to push him off me so he could release my nipples from his dog-like bite. The fight I was putting up must have worked, because he loosened up and directed his attention to another part of my body.

He switched his focus from my breast to my vagina. He began rubbing his strong, immense hand over my vagina, flicking on my clitoris like plastic strings on a guitar, which instantly caused my juices to flow. He inched his head down lower and started sucking around my vaginal area. He knew this drove me wild. After feeling a little more relaxed by his gentle kisses I calmed down and let him continue.

He licked, sucked, and with two skilled fingers, fingered me all at the same time, driving me crazy. I laid there in a complete trance, because he was skilled when it came to oral sex and had me thrown all the way off. I chose not to fight the feelings and emotions that were tearing through every inch of my body and surrendered to the pleasure, allowing him to devour his feast. I covered my eyes with my hands and began crying from one too many emotions building up all at once. I was in total ecstasy and upset at the same time, disoriented, as my feelings continued to confuse me. *Why would he want to eat my pussy if he knew I had just had sex another man?* He wasn't making any sense to me and I didn't want him touching me like this anymore. Not now, not ever.

He rose up, uncovered my hands from my eyes, and wiped away the tears that were streaming down my face. He began whispering in my ear "*I love you,*" and "*I'll never leave you,*" trying to comfort me from the pain and anguish I was feeling.

"Ain't no reason to cry now, Desi. We both messed up and did some bullshit. Now let's kill it and move on, please," he begged.

I closed my eyes and let the tears flow as he rammed his large dick in my already sore walls of my vagina. The way he pounded himself inside of me, hard and emotionless, demonstrated that he was still angry. He made all sorts of loud grunting noises that were turning me completely off. The sounds that escaped his mouth sounded almost animal like while attacking his helpless prey.

He never had sex with me rough like this before, and I for sure didn't like it. There was no pleasure in it for me at all. Cee was definitely turning into something evil and it scared me, because I never knew which personality to expect. He was not the same sweet person that won my heart years ago, but now a deranged maniac that frightened me. He pounded my insides with repeated vicious strokes, like he had a point to prove and needed to teach me a lesson. If I could only find a way to teach him the ultimate lesson he never learned, which was how to love me.

After he finished torturing my vaginal walls, he got up and walked toward the bathroom. He stopped in the doorway with his back still facing me. "Go clean yourself up in the other bathroom. Will's coming over in a minute so we can handle some business, and just so you know, your pussy didn't taste right," he stated seriously, and walked into the bathroom and slammed the door behind him.

He didn't even turn around to look at me, making me feel like a worthless, dirty slut. He slammed the bathroom door so hard that it caused me to flinch, sending chills down my spine. I laid there, waiting, hoping somehow the mood would change, but he didn't even have enough consideration to come back with a cloth to clean up the mess he had made all over my thighs.

Slowly, I sat up in the bed, vagina and legs aching like I had been beaten, and wobbled into the second bathroom to wash him off of me. Under the streams of the steaming hot water, I broke down to my knees onto the cold slippery porcelain tub and sobbed like a baby. Aside from the spontaneous twisted fuckery that just occurred, all that continued to replay in my mind was him saying *your pussy didn't taste right*. And how would he even know when he hadn't touched me in so long? *Could he actually tell that I wasn't only having sex with him*? I didn't know if a man could tell or sense if a girl had been intimate with another man by touch or feel, or if he was just saying that to get a response out of me. I didn't have the energy to continue to ponder over it, and I damn sure wasn't about to ask, because I really didn't care at this point.

After what seemed like an hour long shower, I lotioned my body with my lemongrass body cream, wrapped myself in my terrycloth Victoria's Secret robe, and laid down in my bed, while Cee sat in the living room, loudly playing his PlayStation. I buried my face in my pillow and let out a loud scream as tears once again poured from my eyes.

I always wondered how a person that claimed you were the most beautiful person, had the sexiest body, and loved to death, could hurt you the most. It seems like the person who claims they love you the most tends to cause you the most pain. I loved Cee with all I had, mind, body, and soul. Yet, he was managing to cause me so much pain that I felt like I didn't have much to love with anymore.

With each vivid memory that crossed my mind, the pain grew intensively and plagued my soul with constant jabs at my heart, like a doctor performing heart surgery with no anesthesia. I laid there in pain, wishing that one day he would realize that he was the only one who possessed the power to pull the sword from my chest and end my misery.

Chapter Fourteen

There remained an awkward relationship and distance between Cee and I over the next few days. There were times when we were together in the house and didn't say a word to each other. We were basically just going through the motions, and I was beyond fed up with the silent treatment. I kept myself busy with cleaning and tending to Gizmo, but refused to cook or wash his clothes like I use to, because I didn't feel he deserved it. I wanted him understand that I was fed up with living like this and needed things to change, and soon. I was ready and willing to get away from Cee, some way, because things weren't the same and weren't getting any better. I was convinced there was no way our relationship could be repaired at this point. He wasn't trying, so I couldn't fathom why I should waste my time and energy trying to work things out with him.

I realized I needed my own space, away from the dysfunction in my current home. I asked Shelly to go with me to help me find a new apartment. I needed to set myself up immediately just in case things got worse between me and Cee. Even though I didn't believe he would leave me high and dry, I couldn't risk my livelihood by being naïve. I never knew when he might get in one of his moods and decide to be deceitful for no reason. The way things were going between us, I wasn't sure if he still wanted to be with me from day to day.

Shelly knew of some condos that were very nice and decked off on a dead-end street in Covington. After eating breakfast at Waffle House and my venting about my current situation, we contacted the landlord and went over to check some units out. The location and layout of the condos were perfect for me! The landlord showed me a large two-bed, two-bath, three-story townhouse with a two-car garage that was in move-in condition. The guy who owned the condos didn't make me sign a lease or anything. It was probably because he was too focused on Shelly's double-D breasts to care if I was an eligible renter or not. I gave him nine thousand dollars cash up front that I had conveniently taken from Cee's bank account, to cover the first nine months of the lease in exchange for the keys to the townhome the same day.

Gradually, I began taking a thousand dollars here and there from each of Cee's accounts over the past few weeks and deposited the money into a separate account that I had set up for myself. If he was to leave me, I'll be dammed if he left me high and dry, broke, and looking pitiful. I began discreetly moving small things out of my current place and into my new condo. I told Cee I was giving away clothes I couldn't fit anymore, just in case he cared, which I don't think he even noticed.

Whenever he was away for any extended period of time, I would go to my new condo, light candles, listen to my Corrine Bailey-Rae CD or my new Chrisette Michele CD, dance around, and chill. Music had become my new form of mental therapy which I desperately needed at this moment in life. The solitude allowed me to relax and clear my mind of any foolishness or drama that involved my relationship. I grew to appreciate my private time because it provided me with the necessary time I needed to think about my future and what I wanted to do regarding my relationship with Cee and establishing my own life. I found peace within the quietness and serenity of my new place. Sometimes it worried me, because I knew I could definitely get use to this, but I also longed for the love and companionship that we once shared.

* * * *

One morning as Shelly and I were at my new place hanging floating shelves and pictures on the walls, Cee called and said he needed me to make a run with him later that day. Lately, he rarely asked me to go anywhere with him, so I knew this had to be something really important. He said he needed for me to drive to Dayton so he could make a move and couldn't ride alone. I didn't ask any questions. Instead, I went along with it to avoid getting into an argument about me questioning him again. Plus, I knew I would be getting something nice out of the deal regardless, which would only assist with my decorating expenses.

We left for Dayton around four o'clock that day. I had him pick me from our house, so he wouldn't get suspicious about where I had been all day. He showed up in an unfamiliar truck that I immediately assumed was a rental. I figured he had someone else rent him a SUV for this particular run, because he hadn't mentioned anything to me about it. I didn't bother asking any questions about who he got to rent the truck and why didn't he ask me like he had always done, because like everything else he did that seemed suspicious lately, I didn't care. All I wanted to do was get the ride over with quickly, so I could meet up with Jarvis for our late-night dinner at my new place.

The entire ride was quiet and smooth. Neither of us said too much to each other. I wanted to ask a million questions about our relationship and why he was acting different, but decided to put it aside until after the trip. We rode silently up the highway, while he blasted his Lil Wayne CD and rapped along to all the lyrics.

As we approached the exit after about a forty-five-minute drive, Cee turned down the music and instructed me to empty out my purse and put its contents in the glove compartment. I looked at him strange and raised my eyebrow; he must have been crazy. My exposing the contents in my purse was not in the details of this trip. Before I could object, he shot me a stern look and said for me to just do it. He also told me that I would have to drive back to make everything *look good*. I didn't have a clue as to what he was talking about, but I obeyed like the mannerable little child he treated me like. I was hoping he had changed his mind about me driving back since he drove up, but I didn't care as long as we were safe.

I became very uncomfortable whenever he didn't inform me of where we were going or what exactly we were going to do. I wasn't in the mood to talk to him or get in an argument, so I let the situation rest and enjoyed the ride. Usually, I would be full of questions about this and that. However, since we had been basically giving each other the silent treatment, I didn't feel like going there, especially not now.

He made a couple of calls to someone named Rico and asked him for directions to where we were supposed to go when we got closer to our destination. I had never heard him mention that name before, so I made a mental note to ask him who Rico was later.

"You got your cell, right?" Cee asked after he disconnected his call.

"Yeah, but it's almost dead. Why?"

"Just power it off for now to save some juice. You won't be needing it, but just turn it off anyway."

I huffed loudly and shook my head at his random demands. I didn't feel like arguing or questioning, so I turned my phone off and roughly threw it in the glove compartment with the rest of my things.

His phone rang again. I figured from the conversation he was having that, it was the guy Rico calling back. He said a bunch of "okays" and repeated back a street name, "Gettysburg Avenue."

"You hungry? Rico said he's going to be a minute."

"I can eat. How long did he say and who is he anyway?" I asked, really not wanting to eat much because I was trying to save my appetite for later.

"Some nigga that Will knows from his boy Mark...you know, Shelly's old man." He smirked and looked at me, trying to make fun of my friend, and then continued. "I'm supposed to check out some shit to see what he talking about. We shouldn't be too long."

Cee and I sat in KFC's parking lot and ate some food. It seemed like sitting there eating together actually eased some tension between us. We talked about random stuff and both sang along to the songs that came on the radio, like the Rick James and Tina Marie duet. I was actually feeling a little more comfortable about being in his presence now that we were chilling together and not arguing. A part of me wanted him to take this opportunity to try and mend our broken relationship or try to come to an understanding as to where our relationship was headed, but unfortunately I couldn't muster up the guts to bring it up.

About half an hour went by before the guy Rico called back. Cee and I were so busy clowning around that we didn't even pay attention to the time, or at least I didn't.

"He said give him thirty more minutes," Cee said, throwing his last chicken bone in the box and wiping his hands with his napkin.

"What! Thirty minutes?" I yelled, becoming seriously irritated. It'll almost be seven o'clock and I have a headache. Can we go to Walgreens or something, so I can at least get some Tylenol?" I asked, looking at my watch, hoping that dealing with him and his shenanigans wouldn't make me late for my dinner date with Jarvis.

"Naw, let's just sit tight. I don't even know where a Walgreens is around here."

"They're on every corner," I huffed. "Let's just ride and see, guaranteed we'll find one."

"Naw, just wait. Dude shouldn't be that long," he assured me.

About twenty minutes later, his phone rang again.

"He said he stopped to get some Heinekens and to meet him down the street at Burger King."

"Some Heinekens! Are you serious, Cee?" I was now beyond upset and annoyed by the unnecessary delays. "Why can't they come to us? Fuck that! Who do they think we are? I can't believe you're putting up with this bullshit. This don't seem right to me!" I yelled, irritated with the whole situation.

Cee ignored my rant and drove down a couple of streets from the KFC and pulled into the dark, deserted Burger King parking lot. He backed into a parking space closest to the entrance and waited for about twenty minutes until a brown Monte Carlo SS pulled up beside us. In the meantime, Cee and I had switched seats; he was now on the passenger side of the truck. He got out to meet the guy who had pulled in two spaces over from us. Before getting out, Cee instructed me to leave the engine running, because he shouldn't be that long. I obeyed his orders, leaned my seat back so I could relax, and pressed play on the CD player.

Out the corner of my eye, trying not to look obvious, I observed three guys in the car that pulled up, two more than discussed. The scenario just didn't look right to me, but I didn't say anything. Cee didn't mention any other guys that were supposed to be around to do business except for the guy Rico.

A light-skinned guy got out of the back seat, gave Cee dap, and handed him a Heineken. Cee didn't even drink beer, but I guess he took it anyway to be polite. The guy that was seated in the front seat got in the back of the SS. Cee took a seat in the passenger side, leaving the door slightly ajar with his foot planed on the ground. The light-skinned guy walked to the back of the dumpster on the side of Burger King and, what it looked like to me, took a piss. As he walked back over to his car, he stopped in front of the truck and waved at me like he knew me. I didn't wave back, because this situation was appearing a little too strange for my liking. I didn't know any of these strange men and neither did Cee. Instead, I just sat there vibing to the low tunes of Lil Wayne, observing the scene to make sure everything went okay.

My head was still throbbing from my headache and from the built up irritation of this mess Cee had me involved in. I really needed to take something quick before my temples exploded. I noticed a lit up CVS sign at the end of the street, but it had to wait. I'll be damned if I left my baby with these strangers. I didn't care if I was mad at him or not. I still loved him and I was nobody's fool.

The light-skinned guy that I assumed was Rico never got back in the car, but leaned on the passenger side door that Cee had left open. Noticing the fuel gauge was close to empty, I turned the ignition off to conserve gas until we were ready to go. As time went by, I became even more irritated because it didn't seem like any serious business was taking place. It just looked as if they were bullshitting around, laughing and talking about nothing.

They had been out there talking for about thirty minutes already, and I was beyond ready to leave. It seemed like I checked my watch every five minutes wishing they would hurry up. I leaned back in my seat and closed my eyes hoping to help ease my throbbing head.

A couple minutes later, I heard the engine of another vehicle approaching where Cee's so-called business was taking place. I swiftly sat up in my seat to check out the scene and my boo. An unfamiliar black pick-up truck pulled up in between the SS and our truck, blocking my view of Cee and his companions. A straggly older man exited the truck and slid something underneath his large, dingy white t-shirt. The man then sort of skipped over to the passenger side of the car where Cee and Rico were, my heart began to race a mile a minute then abruptly stopped.

Boom! Boom! Boom!

The sudden blast of gunshots rang out, freezing my senses, one loud blast after another. The noise pierced through my throbbing head with each thunderous shot. I sat there stuck, not knowing what to do. My hands shook in fear. I frantically tried starting the truck, but it wouldn't budge. *How fucking convenient*, I thought to myself. I froze when I saw Cee in distress, running to my side of the truck. My eyes couldn't focus on the scene around me, because my organs couldn't connect or keep up with what my senses were trying to convey.

"Get out of here!" Cee screamed to me with rage in his eyes.

"What do you mean?" I yelled, scared and confused, looking from left to right.

Cee was out of breath as he rushed over to my side of the truck. Desperately, he looked me in my eyes and pleaded, "Baby, just leave! Get the hell out of here! Just leave me here! I'll be okay!"

"Get in the truck, Cee! I'm not fucking leaving you here!"

My eyes grew wide as I noticed blood seeping through his ripped True Religion shirt. It looked as if he had been wrestling a pack of bears, fighting for his life.

He flung the back door of the truck open and snatched a duffle bag from the back of the truck. Midway before shutting the back door, something had spontaneously captured his attention causing him to abruptly stop whatever he had planned. He stood completely still and focused on an image to the right of

126

me with a wide glare of sudden fear in his eyes like a deer caught in headlights. I didn't understand his sudden halt or the dreadful expression that appeared on his face until I felt the pressure of hard, cold steel against the side of my already throbbing head.

Chapter Fifteen

"Bitch, tell him to give us the money," the mysterious scraggly man barked in my ear. He was now sitting in the passenger seat next to me with his gun pressed painfully into my skull.

"What money? What are you talking about?" I cried, confused and scared. I tried to turn my head to get a glance at the strange man, but was unsuccessful.

Cee whispered through the crack of the window, so that only I could hear, never taking his eyes off the man, "You my soldier, right?"

I knew this was serious, because he used to ask me that when we first started kicking it when he was working on the block. I always wanted to be around whenever he was handling his business, so I could be there for him if he needed me. He never took me to handle big business deals, but agreed to let me ride along to make his small stops, so I could feel special and included.

He made it a point early in our relationship to prepare me for any unforeseen situation that might arise, causing him or myself to be in harm's way. Cee taught me to strategize and be on point at all times, to always evaluate my surroundings, and to analyze all activity that took place around me. That way, if something was to jump off, I wouldn't be left standing there looking stupid like a hopeless girl without a clue. He taught me to think at all times and how to remove any weak, spontaneous emotions that may surface to overcome dangerous situations.

Staring directly ahead, as tears began to form behind my eye lids; I slightly nodded in agreement and knew immediately I had to put my game face on. I was in no way, shape, or form prepared for this type of situation to jump off tonight, no matter how proficiently trained I thought I was on how to properly react. I was in total disbelief that this was really happening, and it wasn't a mock trial. There was no way I could live up to being a soldier if I wasn't prepared to fight.

"She don't know shit, man!" Cee angrily yelled at the guy, snapping me from out of my daze.

A single tear dropped from my eye. Not because I was scared, but because I was worried about Cee and what was about to happen next. I knew I would have to leave him here and handle this madness the best I could all by myself, rather I lived or died.

After sucking up my emotions, I whispered a prayer for God's protection and mouthed for Cee to go. He slammed the back door shut and abruptly took off running across the busy street with his duffel bag in tow. Reality hit me that I was now all alone and had to fend for myself against this strange man that sitting next to me with a gun to my head, but I was ready for the games to begin.

The man pushed the gun harder into my skull and demanded that I give him the money. I honestly didn't know of any money or anything else for that matter. I was just as clueless as he was, and that bothered me more than anything.

"Look nigga, I don't know nothing about no money. You're asking the wrong one. I don't even know the dude like that. He just asked me to drive him up here," I stated in a cold tone, never raising my voice. I had to completely changed my demeanor.

I tried to remain calm and hide my fear, so he wouldn't get irate and shoot me.

"Listen, little lady, I don't want to have to hurt you, 'cause you ain't got shit to do with this. You just happen to be with the wrong nigga at the wrong time," he said, lowering his tone and regretfully shaking his head from side to side.

"What did he do?" I calmly asked, trying redirect his attention and stall him from going after Cee. I wanted my baby to be able to get away...far, far away. He released some of the pressure from the gun off of my head allowing me to slightly turn my head.

I noticed the other three guys were still standing around the car arguing among themselves about what went wrong.

"Go get the nigga," the man screamed to the guys when he noticed me looking over in their direction as they all stood by the car bickering about who did what.

Rico jumped in the driver seat and sped off, while the other two guys took off running after Cee.

"Tell me what you know or you're going to have to come with me, lil' mama," the man said, now directing his attention back on me, never letting his steel depart from my head.

"I don't know shit!" I screamed in disbelief. "I don't even know what is going on, and I ain't going nowhere but home. I'm not on this shit!"

"Your friend tried to rob my boy," the scraggly man lied, changing up the story as if I hadn't been sitting here the entire time.

"I'm sorry to hear that, but he was supposed to pay me to drive him up here. Now I'm stuck in this bullshit," I lied, trying to remain innocent and neutral within this fiasco.

The man lowered the gun from my head and looked out the door to see if the guys had caught up with Cee. A sigh of relief escaped my lips, as my mind drifted, wondering if these guys had anything to do with running Cee off the road that night. This was getting too out of hand.

The strange man hopped out the truck and stood in the door watching Rico drive off after Cee. I made a split decision to also get out of the truck and try to make it into the secure premises of the Burger King. I had to get away before he tried to hurt me or force me to go God knows where with him.

As I ran towards the restaurant, I heard two powerful shots in my direction. They startled me, almost making me trip over my own feet dodging any bullets, so I wouldn't get hit. The man took off on foot across the street where Rico was now parked after shooting two thunderous shots in my direction. I began to cry hysterically. All of my hard exterior went straight out the window, because I knew in my heart they had caught up with my baby.

I desperately ran up to the building and banged on the locked door of the Burger King for someone to let me in. The employees were all gathered around, gawking at me through the glass door. I couldn't believe the employees in the restaurant were just standing there looking at me dumbfounded as I banged, pleaded, and cried for them to let me in. A young white guy looked around at his two co-workers and shrugged his shoulders, his face displayed pure sadness as he looked into my eyes. He must have sensed my desperation, because he slowly walked over and unlocked the door.

"Don't let her in here! She can get us all killed," an older black woman shouted to the kid.

"Shut the fuck up!" I screamed, running inside, with tears streaming down my face. "I need to use the phone, please," I said to the kid, as I turned and locked the door behind me.

An older gentleman raised a red phone and said I could use it, but it only made emergency calls.

"Can I call the police for you?" He asked nervously, looking at me up and down.

"No, I need to call my friend. Give me the phone."

I snatched the receiver from his hand and dialed Shelly's number, but got a recording that said the phone couldn't make long distance calls. I slammed the headset and noticed the older black lady speaking softly on her cell phone giving a detailed description of me to whomever she was talking to.

"You bitch!" I screamed, then ran over to the window to see if the coast was clear.

I now had to find a way to get away from here before the police showed up. The SS and the pick-up truck were nowhere in sight. I unlocked the door and ran out of the restaurant back to the truck.

As my emotions escaladed, a thick lump formed in my throat when I noticed streaks of blood outside of the truck that had come from Cee's wound. After jumping inside, I continuously stomped on the gas pedal and frantically turned the keys I had left in the ignition. Thank God it started. As I pulled off, all I could think of was if they had caught my baby, did he get away, or was he dead. Various horrific images flooded my mind causing my panic to increase.

I retrieved my cell from the glove compartment, powered it on, and called Will. I waited patiently as his phone constantly rang until his voicemail came on. I redialed his number and left a desperate message trying my best to explain the situation, skipping over my words in between sobs about Cee's safety and how I was scared to death. I disconnected the call and then called Shelly.

"What up, girl? Why has your phone been off?" Shelly rambled into the phone.

"Girl, Cee got shot and I'm in some bullshit. I don't know where I am!"

My phone beeped alerting me it was about to lose power.

"What!" Shelly screamed into my ear.

"Yes, and I'm so scared. I don't have much time for details my phone is about to die. I need you to get in touch with Will for me and call Cee's mom. Her number is 641-01..."

I looked at the screen on my phone and noticed it had conveniently died on me. *Damn batteries weren't worth shit.*

"Fuck!" I screamed and threw my phone against the dashboard.

As I sped down the dark road, my chest began to rise and fall faster and harder. My breathing was becoming more and more sporadic, and I knew at any moment I was going to lose it.

"Why, God? Why? Please let my baby be okay," I screamed, wiping away snot as it drained from my nose.

The car next to me kept looking over at me like I was a psycho bitch gone mad as I cried and yelled aloud to no one.

"Ohhhh...please don't let my baby be gone. Not like this, Lord. I...I have to tell him...I have to tell him I love him. Lord, please let me hold him one last time, so I can tell him I love him. I'm gonna kill them son of a bitches if they hurt my baby! Oh...baby you don't deserve this...oh shit! What am I going to do without Cee, Lord? Please tell me...what am I going to do? He's all I got. Please don't take him away from me. Protect him, God...Please protect him for me. If you never do anything else for me, just don't let him die!" I pleaded, screaming to the top of my lungs and crying like I had lost my mind.

I glanced at the ring on my left hand and suddenly a sense of hope empowered me, because it reminded me of all the positive times in our relationship. Without him, this ring meant nothing. There was a reason I still wore this ring after all the pain and deceit, and in a personal way, my ring symbolized hope. For that reason, I needed to pull myself together quick, so I could think straight and hope for the best.

I whipped the truck around and made a quick U-turn when I noticed I had driven too far looking for Cee. If they had caught him, they probably beat him to death or shot him up, leaving him in a dark alley somewhere to rot. I couldn't help but think of all the horrible things they could be doing to my baby. Just the thought of him lying somewhere dead made me nauseous.

I sped back down a familiar street towards the KFC and noticed some young boys standing at a corner store posted up. I recklessly pulled up and asked if any of them had a cell phone that I could use. They must have noticed the crazed look on my face or saw the blood on the truck, because no one spoke up.

"Hello!" I yelled to the three mutes.

The tallest one spoke up. "I ain't got no minutes on my phone, shorty."

"Fucking young-ass bums, you at the store! Buy some! What the fuck y'all standing out here for?" I yelled, going off on the young boys for no reason. They hadn't done anything to me, but I couldn't help from lashing out at everyone that possibly crossed my path.

I sped off and traveled back in the direction that Cee and I had come from earlier.

Three police cars sped pass me traveling in the opposite direction with their sirens blaring and lights flashing. I instantly pressed on the break, slowing down and drove as calmly as possible, following the speed limit so I wouldn't look suspicious and get pulled over. I knew they were headed straight to the Burger King to investigate the scene and to search for any remaining victims or suspects.

I noticed my hands trembling uncontrollably as I tightly held on to the steering wheel, realizing how nervous and shook up I really was. I noticed a barely standing payphone on an unlit street as I slowly approached a blinking red light. After illegally parking the truck on the curb, I searched the truck and my purse for spare change so I could make my calls. I came across some loose change from the food we had purchased earlier, which unfortunately only added up to fourteen cents. Since there wasn't enough change for the call, I punched zero for an operator and prayed someone would pick up.

"Can I help you?"

"Yes, I need to make a collect call, please," I replied, weeping into the receiver.

"Do you need some help? Are you okay?" The lady asked with concern.

"I'm okay. I just need you to call a number for me."

Without hesitation, the operator dialed Ms. Marie's phone number for me, and I got the recording that said she didn't accept blocked callers. I apologized to the operator and asked her if she could try to connect me with someone else. I dreaded making this call, because I hadn't dialed this number in about two months, but I knew I could always count on my sister to answer.

"Hello," a sleepy voice answered.

"Hey, Angie, it's Desiree," I said, trying to sound as normal as possible, because I didn't want to worry her.

"Hey, girl. What's up? Just laying down. This baby is kicking my butt."

"I'm sorry to call you so late, but I need you to do me a favor and call Ms. Marie, Cee's mother, for me."

"Okay," Angie replied slowly. I could tell she was confused and wanted to know why I needed her to call Cee's mother for me, but she didn't ask any questions. "What's the number? You all right, girl?"

"No, not really. I just really need you to call her for me, please."

Angie clicked over, dialed Marie's number, and clicked back over with Marie on the line.

"Desiree, what's going on?" Marie asked, suspiciously.

"Marie, Cee got shot up here in Dayton. I don't know where I am or where he's at," I rambled, before breaking down in tears again.

"My baby got what? Oh Lord! Alisha, call Will now! Something has happened to Cee and Desiree is with him!"

I continued on with the details. "I'm on a street called Gettysburg Avenue, but I don't know exactly where. I'm at some payphone. I need help, Marie. I need Cee."

"Go to the police station, Desiree, and calm down, sweetie. I will be there as soon as I can."

"What!" I screamed, confused. "You know Cee wouldn't want me to go to no police station."

"Well, what else you gonna do but get yourself hurt?" Marie shot back, getting angry at me for questioning her authority. "I'm on my way and be safe. Call my cell as soon as you get to the station."

"All right," I replied, even though I was reluctant to go. "Angie, you still there?"

"Yeah, I'm here. Girl, go to the police, for real. I know how you are," Angie said, sniffling and blowing her nose.

"I will. I promise. Please don't get yourself all worked up and upset my nephew. I'm going to be okay. I will call you as soon as Marie gets here. Thank you so much, Angie. I owe you one. I love you, girl."

I started crying harder, because I didn't know what to think or do. I didn't want to get off the phone. I felt safe standing here talking to people I knew loved me.

"I love you, too. You don't owe me nothing but that call, so I'll know you're safe. Bye, Desiree. I love you."

After my sister hung up, I stood there holding the receiver in my hand and remembered the operator was still on the line. She connected me with the nearest police station, which was only a couple of blocks away from where I was located. I felt bad after hanging up with the nice operator. I wish I had gotten her name or information, so I could call and thank her for all her help. She deserved some kind of acknowledgement for her patience and understanding.

Hesitantly, I drove to the police station as I was told, regretting it the entire ride there.

Chapter Sixteen

At a young age, noticing all the corruption and crime officers were involved in around my neighborhood made me not the biggest fan of law enforcement. To make matters worse, the crooked police who were sent to assist me at this station were beyond words. The whole idea that cops were supposed to protect and serve was a total understatement. These police were dirty pigs in human disguise. There wasn't a time where they asked me how I was holding up or showed an ounce of compassion or remorse for the pain that I was enduring after I came in for help. As soon as they associated me with the recent shooting on Gettysburg Avenue, the shady interrogation began.

There was a fat white cop who constantly harassed and yelled at me for no reason about how I knew everything about the drugs. He spat random insults about keeping this ghetto activity in Cincinnati. Then there was an older black, grey-haired cop. I guess he was sent to play the good cop, because he tried assuring me that he would help me out and find out as much as he could about Cee's whereabouts.

I didn't care what they had planned to do to me; they could assume all they wanted. They could have charged me with whatever they could conjure up to try to incriminate me for all I cared. All I wanted to know at this moment was whether Cee was alive or dead.

Becoming enraged with my annoying silence and blank stares, the white man took me into a small room where I sat for almost a half an hour patiently waiting for them to come interrogate me more. I didn't really care or put up a fuss about them leaving me alone in the cold room, because I needed some alone time to think. I knew they couldn't charge me with anything. Plus, I needed time to clear my head and figure out what I needed to say or do for them to let me go without any problems.

The fat white cop returned a short while later, propped his leg against the wall directly across from me, and stared at me for a moment trying to intimidate me. He repeated each question he had asked me previously, but this time twisting his words around to see if my story would change. I was no fool, so he was shit out of luck with his trickery. My patience was wearing thin and I had no intent on telling him anything about what had occurred. I stuck to my story, my friend was shot, and that was all that I knew.

"Sorry sweetness, your story's not adding up. Can you tell me why there is blood on the outside of your SUV and why my guys found over forty thousand dollars in cash in the back of your truck?" The white cop said, as he slowly walked and stood over me with his foot propped up on the bench that I was sitting on.

"You're lying, just for me to tell what you want to hear. And that isn't my truck, Mister," I said, mimicking him. "My name ain't on shit." I turned and lowered my head from the malicious stares of his piercing beady eyes.

"I don't think you would like it when the judge sentences you to do time for being an accessory to a crime involving drugs, money, and a possible homicide, missy. So, I advise that you look me in my eyes and tell me what you know. This time, the truth would help."

The black cop came in and sent the white cop away, thankfully interjecting any further dialogue before it escalated into a verbal altercation. He apologized for his partner's behavior and tried sweet talking me into confessing to whatever I knew about the shooting at the Burger King, the money in the truck, and the drugs.

"Did you hear anything about my friend yet, sir?" I asked, trying remain as calm as possible so I could get him to cooperate with me.

"No, I'm sorry. I'm still working on it, though. Right now, I need you to come with me so you can pick out the guys you said assaulted your friend and write a truthful statement. You're not making yourself look any better with the stuff we found in the back of your truck. I think you know something about the shooting over at the Burger King, also, but I'm not accusing you of anything," he said, faking a sincere smirk on his face.

The cop removed his pager from his belt clip as it started to beep and vibrate loudly.

"I'm sorry, sir, but I can't help you until you help me by telling me the status of my friend. Did you call around to any of the hospitals?"

The cop completely ignored me as he stared at his pager walking towards the door to exit the room. "Let me get this, and let's hope it's good news. You need anything?"

"Yeah, Cee," I replied underneath my breath and lowered my head into my lap.

The cop came back and delivered the news that Cee was at Dayton Memorial Hospital and was in critical condition. He had lost a lot of blood, but thankfully he was alive. I agreed to go with him into a computer room after he gave me Cee's status and picked out random innocent men that could have possibly been the shooter. I repeatedly explained that I was in no condition or mental state to look at random faces and accurately choose any of them. I felt bad for the men and the inconvenience I may have caused them, but at that moment, I didn't care, because I needed to get out of this place so I could get to Cee. I knew they weren't going to let me out until I cooperated one way or the other. I began to wonder where Ms. Marie was and if she had left me for dead. I prayed silently that Marie hadn't forgotten about me and that Cee was going to be okay.

The white cop pressured me to write a statement about what really happened, but I refused to lift a pen until I was able to use the phone to call Marie. The black cop promised that I could use the phone after I cooperated and wrote a brief statement about what I knew. I snatched up the pen and began furiously writing on the yellow notepad.

I don't know why anyone would ask a girl to write a statement under these conditions, but here it is. These cops are dicks, and I tried to tell them I didn't know anything about what they are talking about, but they continuously harassed me anyway. They are some dumb motherfuckers and should be fired. The black dude was cool only because he wanted to seem like the good guy, but he can go to hell, too. I want to get out of here. I came here for help and all they did was make matters worse. Fuck the police, once and for all. The entire force can burn in hell.

Sincerely,

Desiree Natalia Wright

I sat there for a couple minutes to make it seem like I was writing a detailed statement. I then folded the paper in half and demanded my call. I wasn't giving them what they wanted until I was punching numbers on a telephone.

"Your family is waiting for you in the lobby," the fat cop snorted with a smirk on his face. He snatched the paper from my hand just as I was picking up the receiver to place the call to Marie.

I looked at him with total disgust, slowly placing the receiver back on the hook. It took everything inside of me not to knock the shit out of him with the phone. I played it cool and walked away, because I couldn't stand being here any longer.

The black cop unlocked the door to let me out and thanked me for my cooperation. When I saw Marie standing in the waiting room, I greeted her with a tight hug, relieved that she didn't abandon me at the station. She informed me that she had been waiting in the lobby for me for about a half hour because the cops refused to let her come in and see me until they finished questioning me.

"They said you were writing a statement. Is that true?" Marie asked softly.

As I opened the door to leave, I responded, "If you only knew."

We had to stop between two doors that led to the outside of the building for the desk clerk to buzz us out. I welcomed the chill of the air outside as I inhaled and exhaled a sigh of relief. My nerves slightly calmed knowing that Cee was alive and Marie was here to take me to him. The air grazed my skin, causing the tears that had fallen from my face to dry. I heard the white cop yell out, "Fucking bitch," as we exited through the doors. He had gotten his statement, all right.

I sat silently in the back seat of Marie's car as my mind blurred in and out. I was physically there, but mentally I was gone. Visions of Cee's last look of despair, the faces of the assailants, and the blood on the destroyed rental truck reappeared over and over in my mind. The entire ride to the hospital, I sat still with my hands clasped tightly in my lap and kept my eyes tightly closed to restrain the tears that were freely falling down my face. I was thankful that Marie didn't overload me with questions, because I wasn't ready to answer anything at this moment. I just wanted to get to Cee.

The only thing that made me snap back into reality was when I entered Room 223 and saw my baby laying in the hospital bed with tubes everywhere. At that point, I was relieved that he was alive, but inside I was utterly destroyed. I couldn't hold back my emotions any longer and began crying hysterically, thanking God that my love was still alive.

There were detectives lingering around outside the room that tried to get my attention to obtain additional information, but I refused, I was beyond fed up with police. A nice, young Hispanic nurse offered me some pills to help calm me down after noticing how hysterical and shaky I was. She said I could lay down and rest in a separate private room if I needed to get myself together or sleep it off, but I politely declined. I graciously accepted the two small pills and relaxed in the chair directly next to Cee. I stared at him, silently crying until the pills took effect and I drifted off to sleep holding tightly to his hand. I wasn't leaving his side for no one or for any reason, especially not now.

Around seven that morning, I was abruptly awakened by all kinds of beeps and buzzers screaming into my ears. A couple of nurses rushed in and said Cee was coming to and was going into shock. His nurse injected the IV in his arm with something and he instantly calmed down. I sat there wide-eyed and terrified out of my mind. Anything the nurses asked of me, I was ready and willing to assist at all times.

Chapter Seventeen

Cee had managed to make it through after sustaining three gunshot wounds to his stomach and abdomen. He lost about six pints of blood, and underwent two intense surgeries. Both of his surgeries were very successful, but left him very weak and unable to do anything for himself. As the days passed, I came to appreciate how strong of a man he was. I knew it took everything out of him to leave me to fend for myself and knew he wouldn't have made it to be here today if he hadn't gotten away.

I later came to find out that when Cee took off running across the street, he had managed to stop a young girl at a drive through of a Taco Bell across from the Burger King and pleaded for her to take him to the nearest hospital. She had to have been his angel in disguise, because from what I heard, she didn't put up a fuss or anything. She said she sensed Cee's urgency and noticed that he had been injured and drove him directly to Dayton Memorial Hospital, so he could get the professional help which ultimately saved his life.

I never got to meet this girl because Marie said she didn't want to be around when I showed up. She managed to walk away with a nice lump sum of cash for her compassion and kindheartedness. She agreed to keep quiet about the situation and go about her business like nothing had ever happened. I wanted to personally hug and thank her for saving my baby's life, but I figured that this angel didn't seek nor need personal praise, because as she agreed, she never showed back up. Her deed was straight from the heart and for that I was highly grateful.

It took Cee two days to recover from the surgeries and to finally open his eyes for more than a couple of seconds. While he slept most of the day, I either read books that Marie had brought me or sat by Cee's side talking to him. I'm not sure if he heard me or was even listening to me randomly babble, but I wanted to assure him that he wasn't alone. I know I had to have been annoying at times, talking up a storm, and if he could talk, I'm sure he would have screamed at me and told me to shut the fuck up. The mere thought of him saying anything to me at that moment, yelling or not, made me smile.

Marie brought me clothes every other day, and I washed up and changed my clothes at the hospital. My pride and sense of fashion all went out the window; trying to be cute was the last thing on my mind. Every day I would wet a brush, rub grease in my hair, and pull my hair into the neatest ponytail possible. This situation made me realize and value the importance of the people I was blessed to have in my life and how much they really meant to me.

The day Cee fully came to and was aware of his surroundings, he slowly turned his head and saw his mother, Alicia, Will, and me all by his side. We stared at him like he was an alien from out of space that had just touched down to planet earth as he scanned each of our still faces. He tried to talk, but couldn't because of the tube down his throat. It looked as if he was going to choke, so I gently rubbed his head to let him know that it was okay and that we all understood.

He closed his eyes for a brief moment, regained his composure, and silently mouthed 'My soldier' as a single tear expelled from his eye. My heart plunged into my abdomen, and instantly once again I started crying and turned away, ashamed because I didn't feel like a soldier at all. His family may not have known what he was trying to say, but I definitely did. I didn't want him to see me like this. I was a total mess on the inside and out, but I wanted him to know I was holding it together the best I could for him.

I couldn't take it anymore as he struggled to communicate with us. My stomach began twisting and turning like a circus acrobat performing somersaults. Becoming totally overwhelmed by this emotional moment, I ran to the bathroom and violently vomited until my stomach began painfully cramping. Marie knocked on the bathroom door and asked me if everything was okay. I managed to pull myself up and respond that I wasn't feeling very well. I prayed everything had come up, including the pain and depression I was experiencing, so I could get back to being myself again. Lately, everything around me seemed to make me cry or very sad. I was in a permanently depressed state. The only thing that could make me happy again was my baby holding me, laughing, and us loving each other like we use to.

There was little change over the next few days. Nurses and doctors were constantly in and out, and it seemed like they always came up with a new test that they wanted to perform on Cee to make sure he was healing okay. Over time, he became more alert and more and more people came to visit. His mom tried convincing me to leave so I could fully get some rest and real food in my body, but I couldn't do either. I agreed to walk to the cafeteria with Marie and Alicia to give Cee some alone time to chill with his boys, instead of me hovering over him every minute.

He was currently under protective custody because security said there were several strange people calling and asking the staff about a new patient named Cee. They obviously didn't know his real name to obtain any information, so anyone that came to visit had to get approval from Marie or myself. I felt comfortable leaving him this time because Will was there and I trusted him being there more than any of his other friends. Otherwise, I would have stayed and monitored like a watchdog.

* * * *

"What up, man?" Will said to Cee, letting go of the three large get-well balloons he had brought in with him.

Balloons were the last thing he needed in his room to add to the colorful bouquets, balloons, cards, and gift baskets that arrived almost daily. His room was filled to capacity with gifts to the point we eventually started giving away some to the other patients in the hospital who hadn't received any visitors. You would have thought the patient in 223 was someone who had just given birth, not someone who had gotten shot. There was speculation lingering amongst the staff that Cee may have been some sort of celebrity or rapper because of the anonymous callers, all the visitors that were in and out showing love, and the abundance of gifts continuing to arrive.

Cee balled up his fist and slowly moved it back and forth to let Will know that he was still fighting. Will hated to see his boy laid up in this type of anguish and wanted whoever was responsible to pay with their lives or someone close to their hearts. Not wanting his boy to have to relive or deal with what all had happened that night, Will made it up in his mind that while he was in Dayton, he would hit the streets and let them do all the talking.

"Hey man, you know we got you, right?" Will stated, looking towards his three boys that he had brought along with him.

Cee looked over at Jeff who quietly argued with someone on his cell, and then over to Blue and Troy as they stood looking out the large window. Cee nodded at them for coming to pay their respects. They were all shook up seeing Cee like this, so they tried to direct their attention elsewhere while he and Will chatted.

"I see shorty's holding you down for real. She acted like she wasn't budging when we came in here." Will started chuckling, thinking about how protective Desiree was of Cee.

"Yeah, my baby's the truth. Will, I really fucked up, man." Cee said rasping, trying to speak as the pain shot through his chest and throat. He sat there feeling like shit as the pain from his abdomen and his heart attacked him at the same time. He hated the thought that he had to leave his girl to fend for herself. "They could have killed her, bro. Then what was I going to do?" Cee said softly, as his voice began to crack, going in and out.

"She's here, man, so that's all that counts. You know she's a true soldier at heart, and she's been around long enough to know how to hold it down for the both of y'all," Will said, trying to comfort his hurting friend.

"I owe her big time, Will. I don't know what to do, but I have to make this up to her. She don't deserve this shit. I should have never brought her along. I didn't really need her to make the run with me but I missed her and wanted her by my side. Now look at this, look at me," Cee said, tightly closing his eyes to hold back his tears.

"Look, it happened and it's over, Cee. You can't cry over spilled milk. Shit, all you can do now is clean it up now. Y'all together and alive that's all that matters. God does things for a reason, and this may be what y'all needed to bring y'all closer. It may sound like a fucked up way to do it, but hey, life can be fucked up at times," Will said, actually thinking about how Rico was going to be fucked up after he caught up with him.

"You right. I feel ya'. You seen her, though, dog. She looks a hot-ass mess." Cee smiled and began coughing roughly as tears formed in his eyes, thinking about his girl and how she was a wreck.

Desiree definitely hadn't been looking like herself lately. She kept her hair pulled back in a raggedy ponytail and walked around in baggy sweat suits like she was a bum.

They laughed and made fun of Desiree's appearance and then changed the subject to the current events in the streets. Cee was relieved that Will was holding him down while he was away, and Will planned to keep it that way.

"Oh, I forgot to tell you some funny shit. You remember them dudes that ran you off the road that day?"

"Yeah, that was fucked up," Cee responded, not finding anything funny about that night. "Why? What you hear?"

"Man, that was Terra's little brothers. I had my little peoples beat their asses after I found out it was them." Will laughed, remembering how he had his little cousins brutally beat Terra's brothers.

"What the fuck you mean her little brothers?" Cee asked softly, confused. He was cool with them up until recently.

"I don't know why they did it and they wasn't budging. They wouldn't tell me why or nothing, but they did say they didn't know it was you in your Benz. I think they trying to get in the game now, but not for long, 'cause after I had gotten into their asses real good, I took them home and told Ms. Alexander. The shit was too funny, because after I had their little asses lit, they had to go home and receive another beat-down from her. They were embarrassed as hell." Will was bent over in his chair, cracking up in laughter. "On some real shit, though, I think Terra put the little bastards up to that shit 'cause they know better. I told you to stop fucking with that looney bitch."

All the laughs and banter came to an abrupt halt after a slight knock came on the door and a familiar face appeared with a small teddy bear and candy in hand. Shocked, Will looked over at Cee shaking his head and slowly rose from his seat. He walked over to the window where Blue and Troy were and joined in on their conversation.

Cee closed his eyes and prayed he could get this over with quick and peacefully before his family or Desiree returned.

* * * *

At the cafeteria, we ate and talked very little. Marie avoided bringing up the incident that happened. She didn't want me to have to relive my nightmare, although it was plastered all over the Dayton news stations when it happened. Instead, she talked about the new series of events and drama in the streets and advised me to call my sister because the baby would be due soon. The news of my new nephew cheered me up and made me a little happier inside. I felt bad because I had forgotten all about calling my sister. Alicia filled us in on all the false rumors that flooded the streets after the shooting, like how Cee and I were both shot, and how Cee died and the doctors had to revive him. As much as I loved hearing gossip, I couldn't bear hearing rumors about me or my man when people had no idea what the hell they were talking about.

We walked back up to Cee's room after about an hour of chatting and Marie trying to force me to eat more food and drink more water, which only made me sicker. As soon as we entered the room, my blood pressure rose to a critical level at the sight of her standing there with a white teddy bear and a box of candy in her hands.

"What the fuck are you doing here?" I asked, between clenched teeth trying not to be too loud.

Terra flashed Cee a frightened look, and then looked over to Marie for reassurance.

"Get out!" I yelled hysterically. "Get...the...fuck...out...of...here!" I jabbed my finger into Terra's chest with each word I spoke, with vengeance growing rapidly in my heart.

The nurse quickly came into the room to see what the commotion was all about and to see if everything was okay.

"Desiree, calm down," Marie quietly said, pulling me by my arm so the nurse would leave. "Everything is fine." Marie ashamedly looked at the nurse. "She's just under a lot of stress. We can handle it from here. Thank you."

"How did she get in here, Marie? Did you give her authorization to come up here? Please let me know," I cried, feeling betrayed, wanting to know why Terra was standing in my man's room. "Are you with me or against me?" I asked throwing my hands up in the air. "I don't understand this shit." I felt like Marie and everyone else at this moment was against me.

"Baby, it's okay," Cee said in a raspy voice, trying to calm me down. He wasn't supposed to talk much because his throat was still sensitive after the tube had been removed.

"No, it is not! She has to go," I yelled, while roughly pushing Terra towards the door.

As she tried to break free from me, I blocked her like a defensive linebacker. However, she was successful in pushing me to the side with all of her weight, and rushed over and whispered something into Cee's ear.

I snatched her up by her arm and dragged her towards the door. "Naw, bitch, you got to go!" I barked, forcing her out the door and slamming it shut after her.

I couldn't believe the bitch had the audacity to show her face after everything I had went through. I didn't care whose baby momma she was. I was still number one and called the shots around here.

I continuously paced back and forth, trying my hardest to calm down, while the entire room stared at me in disbelief. Will and his boys said their goodbyes and left after the commotion, and Marie and Alisha left shortly after them.

After everyone left, Cee told me to come lay down in the bed with him so I could be next to him. I didn't have the strength to argue about why she came, and I didn't feel it was appropriate to stress him out about anything while he was in this condition. He kissed me softly on my ear as I struggled to get comfortable in the little bed with him. He whispered that he loved me and was going to make everything okay.

I wanted to believe him, but I couldn't. My heart had heard this same ole love song before. I snuggled up under his weak arm and relaxed as the Valium the nurse had slipped me began to take its toll.

Chapter Eighteen

The following week remained fairly quiet and luckily without any unexpected visitors. Cee and I were in the middle of our Tonk game, when he screamed out for me to turn the volume up on the television.

"Hi, this is Valencia Corbett reporting live at the crime scene of a homicide that they are considering the city's most gruesome crime investigation ever. Here I stand with Detective Parker to give us more information regarding this horrendous act of violence. Detective?"

Cee and I dropped our cards and listened attentively as Detective Parker gave details about the murder.

"Unfortunately, the lives of twenty-five year old Sheila Patrick and Roderick Harding were both taken while their sixteen-month-old baby slept in the other room."

Pictures of a petite, young, light-skinned girl with blonde hair alongside a mug shot of Rico flashed on the screen. My heart started beating a million miles a minute after immediately recognizing his face. I covered my mouth with my hand and turned to look at Cee. The expression on his face startled me; he stared at the television like he was going to burn a hole straight through it. I directed my attention back at the screen as the detective continued.

"Please be advised the contents of this crime are gruesome and horrific, and may not be suitable for children." The bald, round detective cleared his throat and continued. "My crew reported that the two bodies were found tied to chairs with massive amounts of debris around their inanimate bodies, all while their little son stood screaming in his crib for his lifeless parents. We are not yet sure how long the two have been deceased or in this condition, but a neighbor this morning reported elongated cries of a baby coming from the couple's home and no sign of the parents in days. The nauseating stench from the Clorox soaked rags, which were tied around the victims mouths, filled the room as the officers entered their home.

"Ms. Patrick was found nude, gagged, and tied with one single bullet wound through the front of her head. Mr. Harding appeared to have had suffered extreme torture from the assailants. He was found severely beaten and almost unrecognizable from the amplitude of the injuries that he sustained. His right hand was completely severed and the other punctured, with sewing needles under the tips of his fingernails. We have not gathered all of the information, but were told that there were other injuries too gruesome to mention on air."

"Whoever committed these hideous acts is obviously deranged, dangerous, and needs to be put away immediately for the safety of the general public.

Unfortunately, we have no leads at this time regarding the perpetrators that committed this awful act of violence and are asking anyone that might have any information regarding this crime to contact the Dayton police department immediately. Thank you."

"Shaun, back to you," the news reporter concluded.

I stared back at Cee stunned and visibly shocked from the appalling details of the murder. He cracked a wicked smile and weakly pulled on me, so I could lie beside him in his hospital bed.

"Looks like we need to celebrate, huh?" He asked, glaring at me with that same devilish look that frightened my soul and started kissing me on the lips.

I couldn't shake the thought of Rico and his girl from my head. All I could think of was the possibility of what could have happened to me if I wasn't fortunate enough to have gotten away that night. I felt bad for Rico's girl, but just like the guy told me that night, she was with the wrong nigga at the wrong time.

"What do you think you're about to do in this bed?" I asked, faking a smile and trying to shake the thoughts of that night out of my head.

Cee covered up his face with his blanket like a little kid playing peek-a-boo. "Surprise me."

I got up, stood by the side of his bed, and lifted up the bottom of his blanket. I then slid my head underneath and moved his hospital gown to the side.

"Surprise, surprise," I giggled, as his eyes met with mine.

He removed his head from under the blanket and moaned in elation after I completely indulged his entire rock-hard shaft into the moist, warm crevices of my mouth. He rested the palm of his hand on top of my head in total bliss and left me in control to do my thing.

It had been awhile since we had been intimate and I was scared to even touch him in that manner, but if he thought he could handle it, I was going to give him the surprise he asked to receive. I had to take it easy on him when he started moaning roughly, loud enough for the unit clerk outside to hear and prepared for the finale, because I knew he wasn't going to be able to take anymore.

Cee never mentioned anything about the death of Rico or his girl after watching the news that day. Actually, I was scared to even bring it up or ask his feelings about it because of his constant nonchalant reaction towards the situation. Truthfully, I didn't want to know if he had anything to do with it, because I couldn't imagine him orchestrating anything so horrible. However, when I put two and two together and remembered who he had on his team, all I could do was shake my head and silently mourn for the lost souls. May they rest in peace.

* * * *

A week later, Cee was released from the hospital, but was to be checked weekly by the visiting nurses. He had asked for an early release because he was tired of being in the hospital and wanted to get back to the comforts of his own home. The doctors said he had recovered very well after the intense trauma and losing so much blood. They commended him about being so healthy and strong, telling him to keep up the good work with his progress. He was to follow up with his primary physician in Cincinnati in three days and comply with all of the doctors' orders.

I was happy we were finally able to leave the hospital, even though no one asked me to stay there in the first place. I was still on the verge of a nervous breakdown, while Cee couldn't really remember anything that had happened over the past weeks. I didn't consume myself with any further thought regarding the shooting, Terra, or Rico, because I was elated that my baby was finally able to come home.

I had an ample amount of time to do some serious soul searching and thinking over the weeks while I was by Cee's side. I made up my mind that I needed to get away from this life. I had been through too much in my twenty-three years and was too young to have this kind of damage done to my heart and my mind. I couldn't imagine my life without him before, but this time, we had come too close to us separating permanently, and that scared me. I told Cee that I would always be there for him, but honestly, I didn't want to be a hustler's girl anymore.

The day of his release, Marie and I rode in the elevator as the nurse pushed Cee in a wheelchair along with us. He made sure he was fresh to death, exiting the facility like he was a real superstar. He had asked Will to bring him some appropriate clothes to step out in because he wanted to feel like himself once he got out, not looking helpless in a hospital gown.

As soon as we stepped off the elevator, we were approached by two uniformed officers standing in the main lobby. My vision blurred and instantly I started feeling lightheaded as the officer began speaking directly to Cee.

"Cleveland Thomas, you have a warrant out for your arrest," was all I managed to hear before passing out on the cold, hard-tile floor.

* * * *

The events that took place over the next month turned my world completely upside down and created drastic changes that I was not at all mentally prepared to handle. The courts had temporarily seized the condo that Cee and I shared and froze all the accounts in his name. Good thing I had thought two steps ahead and kept my condo in Kentucky and put money up for myself to fall back on in case anything like this were to happen.

Cee was charged with some petty driving charges and probation violation that cost him one year in a minimal security prison. The police had been on his tail trying to conjure up anything they could against him to put him away for longer, but they were unsuccessful. I knew they felt stupid that they couldn't get what they really wanted and wasted their time, because all they got was a measly year out of him. We later found out the FEDS were actually ones who ran up in our townhouse. They said someone called and reported that we had guns in the house, which was a complete lie.

The bad news for me was that I found out I was about two months pregnant and didn't have a clue by who. This information messed me up more than anything.

I parked Cee's Range that I was now allowed to drive across the street from Justice Center. Never having done this before, I was nervous as hell. Today was the first day I could manage to come visit Cee because I was trying desperately to get our lives back in order. I hadn't mentioned the pregnancy to him because I felt I needed to tell him in person; today was the day.

While checking in with the guard and signing the wooden clipboard, I noticed he already had a visitor who was still there. The guard told me that his sister was still visiting and I could join them if I didn't mind. Not caring, I agreed to go along with the visit, so I could get this over with. As I approached the visiting room, my heart raced, and my hands began to tremble, both anxious and nervous. I walked to the guard's booth and was told where I could find Cee, but I didn't see anyone there. I looked around for Alicia's fire-red hair, but didn't see her either. I then saw him sitting there behind the thick glass, and the butterflies in my stomach began fluttering like crazy.

"Terra?" I asked unsure, squinting my eyes, with a slight attitude and my hands on my hip.

She swiftly turned facing me scared to death, with the phone receiver still to her ear and a little boy on her lap. She held the little boy tight to her chest and sat there silently in shock without moving a single part of her body.

I walked and stood directly behind the frightful Terra so Cee could see that I was there. He jumped to his feet so fast that he knocked his chair over when he realized it was me that had Terra looking like she had seen a ghost. He dropped the phone from his ear and stood there filled with guilt, embarrassment, and sadness in his eyes.

They both were shocked to see me standing there and just stared at me, waiting for my reaction. A single tear rolled down my face. I gently laid my hand on Terra's shoulder and calmly told her that she could continue her visit. I then mouthed to Cee, "I'll write." There wasn't anything more he could say or do to justify this situation. I pushed the button to the elevator and turned my back without saying another word. I left feeling crushed, but finally awakened to the truth.

I had to be the bigger woman and walk away for my unborn baby's sake. Those days of going off without thinking had to cease, because it wasn't all about me anymore. I was now living for myself plus one, minus one. I couldn't help but replay that evening in my head after I had the altercation with Terra at the hospital. Cee said to me that he was going to make everything better after he came home, but as far as I could see he wasn't starting off on the right foot.

After briskly rushing to the truck barely containing my tears, I made it official right then and there: Cee and

I were over. This was the perfect time for me to break free and build a life of my own. I couldn't be selfish anymore regarding Terra and her child. If Cee was that child's father, then he deserved to have that relationship with his son. I forgave Terra, also. I couldn't be mad at her when it was evident that he wanted her there. She was young, naïve, and just going off of whatever he was feeding her, and no matter how hard I tried, I couldn't change that either.

As I drove away from the Justice Center headed to no place in particular, my spirit went through an emotional battle. I wanted to be strong and say fuck him and her, but the softer side of me wanted to bust out into tears. I loaded my Notorious K.I.M. CD for inspiration, skipped to track number twelve, and sang along with the lyrics to *Don't Mess With Me* as tears streamed down my cheeks.

"Memories is all it brings when I look at my ring, and "Heartbreaker" is the song I sing."

That song led me straight to the tattoo parlor to get those exact words permanently tatted on my flesh. I needed to be reminded of this relationship for the rest of my life. This would be my lesson for the future to let Cee be the first, last, and only nigga to break my heart.

* * * *

I wrote Cee a couple of letters over the first month, then ended up running out of things to say. I put a couple hundred dollars of the money I had taken from our accounts on his books and decided to call it quits.

Jarvis and Chris were both very understanding of my situation and assisted me in every way they could.

Cee had the nerve to write me a letter about how sorry he was and how he wanted us to be a family again, typical jail syndrome. He took the cake when he told me that he wanted me to meet his son. That shit put me on the verge of insanity, but I kept it cool for the sake of my own child. If he only knew I didn't want to see his child, and little did he know he didn't ever have to worry about seeing mine. He explained that Terra was at the jail because he had to get some things settled with her so he could get his paternity test. That way, he and I could move forward with our lives. I struggled with wanting to believe him or not, but decided against it because men managed to think of some slick shit when trapped behind prison walls.

He also added in his letter that he knew about Jarvis and Chris and all the things we had done. He said he forgave me because he guessed he deserved it. He knew all types of facts that only the people who were there would have known. This messed me up big time because the only person who knew all these intimate details about me would be Shelly. I couldn't physically handle reading the rest of the madness, so I put the letter away and made a mental note to confront Shelly about it later.

Chris had offered to pay for me to stay in an apartment in Atlanta until I decided what I wanted to do regarding my life with the baby. I was ready and willing to leave immediately after he offered, but I had to get with Shelly first and conclude my relationship with Cee. Just in case I needed to return for any particular reason, I paid my rent up for the next year and placed all my belongings in a storage unit. I was sad to go, but happy to finally have the courage and opportunity to rebuild a new life elsewhere.

After packing my final suitcase, I sat and wrote Cee a final letter.

February 23

What up, Cee? I hope all is well. I know I haven't written you in a while, but I've been kind of busy lately. I will be going away for a while, so I guess this will be my last letter. I gave the truck to your mother and gave her the money you asked for. It was about five thousand short, but I'll let you and Will handle that. She told me that her house had been broken into three times since you've been away, but luckily, no one was home. I let her know that she could call me if she needed anything. I left her ten thousand to hold her over for a while to try and compensate for some of the stress she has been through with us.

I found the guy to claim the condo and he vouched that it was his, so it was settled. He told me that he sub-rented the condo to Alicia, not you. So, she took over the condo and is staying there taking care of Gizmo for me. I went ahead and paid the rent for a couple of months so she wouldn't have to worry about making any payments for a while.

You offended me with that last letter talking about meeting your son. It really hurt me to the core. I don't want to meet him. That's your son, not ours. I want you to be there for him, though, because he deserves it. He didn't ask to be here, so you two need to raise him appropriately.

As for me, I'm good, and I'm hoping I can move on and get myself together. I have a psychologist, and she has been helping me to get myself in order. I want you to take care of yourself, and I hope you are healing well. I will continue to pray for you, and I will always love you.

P.S. I wanted to tell you when I came to visit you that day that I'm expecting a child soon, but the baby's not yours.

Take care,

Desiree

* * * *

Out of all the things Cee and I had been through, the toughest thing for me to deal with was confronting Shelly. I couldn't believe my home-girl since we were kids would turn on me. All sorts of thoughts ran through my mind trying to figure out why she would betray me and discuss my business to anyone. I didn't know if her big mouth had got the best of her, if she was trying to impress Will by telling him my business, or if she was jealous of me and Cee. My mind was on a rampage. After I received that letter from Cee, I sat around and worried myself about what I was going to say to her, because besides being upset, my feelings were beyond hurt.

I continuously put off making the call because we had never seriously got into it, and I wasn't the type to make up and ignore the situation like it had never happened. This was some foul shit, and she definitely needed to be called out on it. I was actually nervous calling her, but it had to be done and she needed to be put in her place.

"Shelly, what's up? You busy?" I asked, calmly, trying to mask my anger.

"Shit, girl, chilling. How's the baby coming along?"

"The baby's cool, but I need to talk to you. You got a minute?"

"Yeah. What's up?"

I got straight to the point, now with an attitude and bass in my voice. "Why did you tell Cee my business?"

"What you mean? I ain't talked to Cee since I came to see y'all in the hospital, and you were right there. What are you talking about?"

"Well, somehow he knows everything about Jarvis and Chris, which is information that only you would know. Or did you tell Will thinking he wouldn't tell Cee?" I asked, with a straight attitude, trying to figure out her motive.

"Look, Desiree, don't call me accusing me of shit. I know you emotional and all, but you need to calm down with all this nonsense."

"Naw, I'm cool." I continued. "I just know how you talk and how bad you want Will, or maybe you want Cee. I don't know, but that's fucked up, Shelly. I trusted you and you had to go run your big-ass mouth."

"Look, I don't have time for this. Do what you do. If you wouldn't have done all of this shit behind his back, there wouldn't be anything to talk about. So, fuck you, Desiree. Guess your guilty conscious is getting the best of you after all." Shelly chuckled and continued. "Don't call me with this bullshit. I got more important things to take care of."

Click.

"Bitch," I screamed into the phone as I heard the dial tone.

I slammed down my phone and lowered my head on the table, upset and on the verge of crying. Not just because of her betrayal, but how she was so nonchalant about me finding out. I then called Jarvis and left him a message telling him that I was leaving and would call him when I got to Atlanta.

Growing with rage at every thought and emotion in my head, I picked up my phone and began to call Shelly again to cuss her out, but decided against it. I loved that girl, and deep in my heart, I still did. We were like sisters, but this pain cut deeper than the betrayal of Cee. I just couldn't understand why, and I still wanted answers; however, now wasn't the time. I was looking forward to starting my new life and leaving all the backstabbing, bullshitting-ass people behind me.

* * * *

"Now boarding first class, our medallion members, and anyone with small children or those needing assistance," the agent said over the loud speaker.

I boarded the plane hoping to never have to look back on my past again, but to start anew, building my future in Atlanta. Living anywhere at this point in time had to be better than Cincinnati. I had overstayed my welcome here in this grimy city and it was past time for me to move on.

My pregnancy and unborn child provided me with hope and determination I didn't possess before. There was no way I was going to raise my child in the same type of environment I had grown up in, thinking that type of lifestyle was cool. I wasn't about to have my child grow up to be a hustler like his dad or a woman that depended on men like her mother. It was about time for me to start surrounding myself with people that could help me excel in life so I could find out who I was and what I wanted for myself. I wanted to be an inspiring mother and be able to have my child look up to me and say, *my mom went through some crazy stuff in the past, but she came out on top*. So, the top was where I was headed for the sake of me and my child.

I realized it was going to be difficult arranging a totally different life for myself without my two backbones. With the new transition and taking care of the baby, I knew wasn't going to be in the mood to make new friends because no one could replace all the crazy memories that Shelly and I shared. I was grateful for Chris, but realized that no one would have my back like Shelly or Cee.

I sat in my first-class seat and shielded my watering eyes with my oversized, black Christian Dior sunglasses, as the flight attendants passed out drinks and blankets to the surrounding passengers. No matter how hard I tried to fake it, I was hurting, and at that moment, I wished I was Dorothy from The Wizard of Oz, so I could click my red Sergio Rossi pumps three times and recite "There's no place like home." I surrendered to my tears and allowed them to flow, hoping they would wash my past away.

Chapter Nineteen

The Flip Side of Love...

Atlanta started out wonderful. Thanks to Chris I met some very influential African Americans who showed me that it was possible to move on and become successful after living the street life. Chris and I remained close, but decided to not be exclusive so we wouldn't feel obligated to each other. He insisted that I needed space so I could heal and to figure out what I wanted out of life outside of a man. I went out on a couple of dates, but couldn't take men too serious because of the pregnancy. I wanted Chris to be there for me like he had been before, but he was becoming more and more distant every day. Even though I was gaining a little weight, I tried to look as cute as possible for him whenever we did go out to try and get some kind of affection, attention, or anything out of him, but he didn't seem interested or impressed. I spent hundreds of dollars on maternity clothes just to feel like my old self again. Although it was rough, I needed to realize that my life was longer going to be the same with a child arriving in a few months.

His lack of attention and my decreasing self-esteem led me to constantly think about Cee and our past relationship. I wondered if there was any way I could have mended our relationship or patiently waited things out until after he found out about his son. Now that I was in a similar situation, being pregnant, I was learning to take other people's feelings into consideration. I loved Cee so much, and I would be willing to take him back even now. I needed and craved that love he use to show me to lift my spirits again because I was feeling very low about myself lately.

I wanted to write another letter to him, but I couldn't think of anything to say after the last letter I wrote. I would sit and write letter after letter, and ended up ripping them up, unable to find the right words to say to try to make a wrong situation right. What could I possibly say? *Oh, I'm sorry now that I realize how much you meant to me. And there's a possibility the baby could be yours. I was just too ashamed to admit it, only saying it wasn't yours out of anger.* No way! I knew that would only make him hate me more, so I decided against it and called Jarvis. I got his voicemail again like every other time when I had called. Something fishy was going on with him, so I hung up and called Chris, no answer.

Since being pregnant, my hormones raged and I craved sex like never before. Chris and I hadn't been intimate since I had moved down here, which was strangely odd after reminiscing about all the wild nights we shared in the past. I came to the conclusion that he had to have a girlfriend somewhere around in the surrounding area. That had to be the reason why he got my apartment so far away from his home and why he had been spinning me ever since I got here.

I called Chris again later that evening when I happened to be conveniently in the same area where he lived, driving around with too much time on my hands. Someone answered his phone but didn't say anything. I said hello about three times after they answered and the phone disconnected, I called right back. This time, a female voice answered the phone talking about *Johnson's residence.*

"Who is this?" I asked, wondering if this was the mystery girlfriend answering his house phone, because even when I was there I didn't answer his home phone.

"This is Teresa," the woman smartly replied. "Who is this?"

"This is Desiree. Where is Chris?"

"He is out picking up his friend. Should I tell him to call you when he returns?"

"Yeah, do that," I replied smartly and hung up the phone.

I decided to leave the situation alone and head back to my condo before I raised my blood pressure and risked putting my baby in harm. It was way too early in my pregnancy to be going through this type of drama all over again. The suspicion stayed on my mind all night, though, and I couldn't shake that woman's voice. Something just didn't seem right and the thought of what if nagged at my brain wanting to find out more.

Being nosy and letting my curiosity get the best of me, I couldn't let it rest. I didn't care if I wasn't his girl or if he wasn't having sex with me at the current time, there still was a level of respect that had to be maintained. After all he offered for me to come here. After my first OB appointment, I had done my calculations and realized that there was a strong possibility my child could be his, so I had the right to investigate.

As I laid in my bed watching TV, I looked over at the clock and noticed that it was now one o'clock in the morning, and I still couldn't sleep. So many thoughts racing through my mind, so I got out of bed, got dressed, and hopped in my car. I decided to take a drive to clear my head, which let me straight to Chris's house. My ultimate destination.

Chris always left a spare key under a little frog statue in front of his garage. So, I quietly tip-toed around his house, retrieved the key, and let myself into his large home. There was loud jazz music playing upstairs, so I knew he wouldn't hear me as I entered the house. I keyed in the alarm code and stood at the bottom of the steps listening for voices. My heart raced a mile a minute, pumping with anxiety to know what was going on and to see who was up there.

Softly, I crept up the stairs, eagerly wanting to see if Chris was with this Teresa chick. I peeped through the crack of his bedroom doorway and immediately had to brace myself on the door frame to try and prevent myself from passing out. I was stunned and utterly shocked at the nauseating sight before my eyes. I kicked open the door with my foot like I was the FEDs making the bust of the century, as Chris was delectably engaging in a threesome with a woman and a man!

I stood gawking at them in disgust and even more perplexed than the three stooges that were now staring directly at me. I couldn't believe what I was seeing. I actually caught him in the act of getting fucked by some buff white man while he was eating this chick's pussy. I went wild. I was totally disgusted as my stomach turned inside out. At that moment I hated myself for even messing with this freak in the first place. I tried taking his head off by throwing anything in his room at him that was within my reach. He had to feel my wrath.

He was so embarrassed and shaken that he ran into his master bathroom trying to doge the flying items that came crashing around him. He locked himself inside like a bitch, while his other compadres remained apprehensive in the bed waiting to see if my tantrum would cease. He kept yelling out for someone to call the police, but I dared for any one of them to lift a finger. Just then, I started feeling sharp cramping pains in my stomach. I swiped all the items off his dresser, defeated, and broke down to my knees. Hysterically, I screamed to the top of my lungs and pounded on his wooden floors, hurt, embarrassed, and once again feeling stupid. I weakly tried standing back up and pounded on the bathroom door, trying unsuccessfully to get Chris to come out and face me.

I breathed heavily in and out trying to calm down and ration with him to unlock the door. I tried to ignore the sharp pains as they grew sharper in the pit of my abdomen. Deciding to leave the situation alone for the moment, I braced myself on the bathroom door, bowed over, and cradled my cramping stomach. I kept quiet sitting by the bathroom door to make Chris think I had left, but really I was only waiting to see if the excruciating pains would go away. The lady slowly got out of the bed and approached me with caution.

"Sweetie, I'm sorry. Are you okay?" The naked, tall, lanky, dark-skinned lady asked me.

"Get the fuck away from me, you freak!" I roared.

She put her hands up and stepped back as I buckled over in pain.

"Do you need some help? I'm a nurse. I can help you," the lady said, trying to rest her hand on my shoulder.

I whipped around like I was the possessed girl in the The Exorcist and pounced on her like a wild cheetah. I climbed on top of her and maliciously beat her face in until the white man came over and peeled me off of her.

When I stood up, trying to catch my breath, I noticed blood running down the side of my leg. I knew I had fucked up. I ran down the stairs, got into my car, and rushed myself to the nearest hospital. During the entire ride, the sharp cramping pains intensified and I feared for the life of my child. I prayed to God that he would protect me and my child, promising that I would straighten up and do right if he got me through this.

The hospital admitted me right away and began running numerous test and drew so much blood I thought I was going to faint. The doctor later announced that I had miscarried. If that news wasn't bad enough, he also informed me that there were police waiting for me once I was discharged. Chris had called the police and they put a warrant out for my arrest for assault and trespassing. I lost the baby and almost lost my mind in Atlanta for dealing with a down low nigga. I was more upset at myself than at Chris, because I ended up causing myself to have a miscarriage when I was supposed to be worried about my child and not some man.

Punk ass, I thought to myself. How was he going to press charges on me for coming into his house and putting my hands on that woman when they deserved it and caused me to lose my baby?

After I was finally released from the hospital, I turned myself in to the Atlanta police department. Jarvis was there like my knight in shining armor to rescue me and hired a lawyer to immediately settle my case. I was fortunate that he was there, because every time I called him from the hospital he didn't answer. I left several desperate messages giving minimal details about the incident, pleading for him to come help me. I told him that I had to turn myself into the police soon and that I needed him there to get me out.

It didn't matter if he had been screening his calls or had a new love interest, because like always, he was there for me when I needed him.

Chapter Twenty

Chris dropped the charges against me, but requested a restraining order to be in place to keep me from coming back and having another altercation with him. Jarvis convinced me to pack up my things and leave Atlanta before I felt the need to jump on Chris again. I couldn't stand the thought of returning back to the condo that I had shared with Cee because I hated feeling like I was going backwards. I also didn't want to be alone enduring the silence and loneliness of my place in Kentucky, but I had no other choice. I had no friends left to call on besides Jarvis, and that only added to my sadness.

After settling back into my place in Kentucky, I found myself in tears day in and day out in depression because I wanted my old life back. I couldn't let it go from my heart that I was the one and only cause of my baby's death. The doctor informed me that my miscarriage was probably related to the stress that I was currently enduring and that I needed to relax and remove the stress factors from out of my life. I figured this was God's way of telling me that having a child under my circumstances was not healthy for me or a child, and losing it was the wake-up call I needed to start appreciating my life.

I resented my mother for never teaching me how to live independently outside of a man. I knew she couldn't teach me a life she knew nothing about. Even now, I wanted her to want more for herself. I knew if I were to have a little girl, it would be my goal to learn everything I could to teach her how to be a strong independent woman. Sadly, I never possessed the drive to finish college or have a career of my own because that was never installed in me as a child. The streets provided me with the education and common sense to survive. The emotional high and the thrill of fast money captured my attention from day one, since then that was the life that I had longed for. Finally, I was ready to venture into something new, a change, but unfortunately I had no clue what it was.

I figured the only way I was going to come out of my depression was to get out of the house and surround myself with different things. I began frequenting clubs and bars to get out the house and get attention from men, not always the right type of attention, but any attention at this point was better than the misery I was putting myself through at home.

I became a part-time alcoholic after losing my baby, which only masked the pain I constantly felt inside. I ended up meeting a guy at bar named Maurice that was a straight smooth talker. He approached me with one thing on his mind...sex...and was willing to pay for it, too. I had never accepted money for sex before, but I knew I needed to start making some fast money somehow, especially since the money I had saved up was constantly dwindling.

Maurice was tall and dark just like Cee, but his eyes were the bait. He had these funny looking light brown eyes that didn't fit his face at all, but looking into them seemed to put me in a trance. He also possessed this sexy cockiness mixed with a touch of arrogance, which made him stand out from the rest of the lames that were too scared to speak up. That wasn't the only thing that made him stand out. His jewelry alone could light up a Christmas tree. He possessed all the right characteristics that got me going, and I was ready and willing to take the ride.

My typical way of getting over someone or something was to replace it with something similar to what I already had to fill that void. That's why most of the time when females leave an abusive relationship or unhealthy situation, we seem to end up in another when all we're trying to is was get away and start anew. However, the arms that we run into seem to be very similar to the ones from our past. Not letting go but replacing usually leads us right back into the same circumstances from before. We rarely allow ourselves the necessary time to properly heal or get over the hurt before moving on to someone new. That person may have the same positive attributes as the ex, but can also possess the same negative qualities you were trying to get away from. It may just be that bad boy edge that keeps most females intrigued and keeps us coming back.

I figured I would kick it with Maurice to see what else he was about, and thankfully, he turned out to be all right, or so I thought. He said he only came at me like that because girls these days would only talk to men if they offered money upfront. I wasn't familiar with the game nowadays and wasn't ready to entertain it because I still wanted to be back in the comforts of my Cee. I took my chances with Maurice anyway and chilled with him regularly because he helped me out from time to time, but I never had sex with him. Since I was still mentally disturbed because of Chris's punk ass, I was on the watch for all homo thugs lurking in the streets, every man was now skeptical in my eyes.

He pressured me constantly about letting him come over to my place, but something about my old ways stuck with me. No visitors allowed, except for close friends or family. He openly invited me into his decked out home, probably to show off, but the vibes I felt when I was inside led me to believe this wasn't actually his home. He claimed he owned this four-bedroom, three-bath, three-story home that was equipped with a home gym, theater room, and outdoor pool. I assumed he had money, but not to that degree. I often wandered the rooms when he wasn't around to see if there could be any evidence to add to my suspicion, and like I figured, there were definitely a few that stood out.

For instance, the bedroom that was set up for a teenage boy with posters plastered on the walls of all the latest celebrities. He claimed it was his little brother's room that he had set up for him when he came to visit from his step-parents' house. *Okay, whatever.* Then there was the master bedroom that was decked out with his and hers everything. Candles, oils, and lotions were all around the room like a female had to have decorated. I picked up a picture off the dresser and stared at the forty-something-year-old woman who looked like she could be Maurice's mother. She was the same woman that was actually in all the pictures around "his" house to be exact, and none of them were with Maurice or even of Maurice. He confirmed she was his mother and they were very close and that's why her portrait was sitting on the middle of the dresser, but she didn't live there. I kept thinking to myself, *yeah, right.*

The grand finale to his lies were of course in the bathroom. There in the bathroom was an extra-large purple silk robe, matching slippers, shower cap, and female products under the bathroom sink, which led me to believe this was his parents' house and he was fronting like it was his. I wasn't about to bust his bubble and ruin my funds, so I let him keep thinking that I was born yesterday. I just shook my head at the lameness of this entire situation but decided to along with it.

That incident alone confirmed that I had been out of the game for way too long and wasn't ready to get back in. Dating nowadays wasn't the same. You had to be on the watch for everything from the bisexuals, to the liars, to the fake, fronting-ass niggas.

All the wrongdoings of other men only led me back to my first love who I knew everything about and didn't have to worry about the extra bullshit that came along with the game, my Cee.

Chapter Twenty-One

Coincidentally, I had left Atlanta and was properly settled back in my place just in time for Cee's release. He was being released three months early because of good behavior. I begged and pleaded for Marie to let me pick him up when he got out, and thankfully she agreed. I knew I didn't need to be within a fifty mile radius of Cee, but my body craved him. His touch, his smell, his laugh, his love, all consumed my thoughts daily. I needed just one more time to try and make things right. I didn't know if he would be happy or upset to see me when he walked out of those doors, but that would be something I would have to find out when the time came.

Marie let me use Cee's truck to pick him up, and it felt good just being in something familiar that was his. If he wasn't happy to see me, I knew he would be happy to see his baby all shined up and sparkling. The tint on the truck allowed me to feel a little more comfortable, because he wouldn't be able to tell I was the one picking him up until he got in. I knew I would need time to compose myself and hide the excitement and emotions of seeing him again before he got in the truck. I was nervous and excited at the same time. The moment I saw him walking through the doors, I began saying a prayer to the Lord for Cee to forgive me.

"Hi Cee," I uttered nervously, smiling with embarrassment and excitement flooding my body as soon as he opened the passenger side door.

"What you doing here?" He asked, not returning the excitement.

"I asked Marie to let me come pick you up so we could talk. I missed you, Cee. Can I get a hug, a kiss, or something? Damn."

He didn't budge, but asked me to go to the nearest gas station so he could get something to drink. We rode in complete silence the entire way to the gas station. All types of thoughts went through my mind as we sat there, but I was too afraid to say anything to him unless he broke the silence first. I sunk down into the seat of truck as he entered the gas station feeling defeated and struggled to contain my tears. Not only was I embarrassed, but ashamed of the way that our first encounter in months was unfolding. In my mind I had envisioned him shocked, but overcome with joy that I was there. I hoped that he would wrap his arms around me and embrace me with the love that had been missing from the time we were apart. Unfortunately I was sadly wrong. I had lost his heart and felt from his coldness that his love was gone. Once he returned back to the truck, he told me to move to the passenger's side so he could drive his own vehicle. I remained cool and tried to spark up a conversation with him, but he remained dry.

"Where do you want me to drop you off at?" He asked without looking in my direction.

"At our house. You don't have to go to your mom's. I have a townhouse for us in Kentucky."

"The same one you had before?" He asked sarcastically, and cut his eyes to look at me.

How did he know about my townhouse? I thought to myself. *It had to be that damn Shelly.* I tried switching the subject before he started asking more questions that I didn't want to answer. "You know me and Shelly fell out. I don't talk to her anymore."

"You got the rest of my money with you?" He asked, ignoring my comment about Shelly.

"What money? I gave it all to your mom."

"Naw, that fifty Gs I had you put in that savings for me."

"I thought you gave that to me because it was in the account with my name on it," I replied, looking dumbfounded because the account was now down to under fifteen thousand. "I'll give you what I have left. I'm sorry. I didn't know. Look, Cee, I want us to start over and try to make this work," I pleaded.

"Where's the kid; you don't look pregnant to me."

I lowered my head, feeling a sense of sadness at the mention of my lost child. "I had a miscarriage, and it's a long story that I don't want to talk about."

"Sorry to hear that. I'm going to see my seed today, so I'll get up with you later. I'm going to get a new cell, so call my mom around seven if you want the number."

"So are you gonna come over?" I asked, sounding desperate.

He pulled up to my townhouse to drop me off and blankly stared at me before speaking, "We'll see."

I knew he made that last comment about his son to try and upset me and to get back at me for what I did, but I just took it with a grain of salt. I wasn't going to let him get to me. My new focus now was to come up with a fast way to make up the money I had spent to give back to Cee immediately. I needed money to be the last concern on his mind regarding his faith in moving forward with me.

* * * *

After Cee dropped me off, saying nothing more than, "We'll see," I immediately ran upstairs and called Maurice. I cut straight to the chase and desperately asked him if he knew of any way I could make some quick money besides stripping or having sex. He said he had a couple of girls that made runs for him every now and then, and one just got dismissed. He said I could do a couple of trial runs to see how it went and to make sure I was up to it. I was excited and thankful that Maurice came through, but I also knew he was going to expect something from me in return.

Cee never came that night. I called and got his new cell number from Marie, but every time I called, he didn't answer. He neglected to set up his voicemail when he got the phone, so I took the pleasure in setting it up for him. I made the access code the day I had my miscarriage so he would never be able to guess it.

191

I was lonely living back in Kentucky, all alone again with no Shelly or Cee. I guess Jarvis had also met someone special, because every time I called, he told me he would call me back, but never did. I could tell he was trying to distance himself from me and my drama, and I couldn't blame him. Bored, lonely, and curious, I sat up checking Cee's voicemail almost every five minutes to see if he had any messages from any females, but he never did.

Cee shocked me when he came knocking on my door the next morning unannounced with breakfast. I didn't know if this was his way of warming up to me or if he just figured I was hungry.

We ended up having sex that morning which didn't feel the same to me at all. There was no passion in it like it used to be; I assumed it was because we had been apart for so long, and didn't have the same feelings towards each other as before. It was a sad feeling, desperately trying to fix and change something that has undeniably died, believing that one day something beautiful could possibly bloom. I knew deep in my heart that he loved me, but I couldn't tell if he was still in love with me. Still, I vowed to stick around and try to mend this relationship the best way I could.

After we both woke up from our nap, he asked me for the access code to his new cell, which I denied knowing anything about. I wanted to keep track of him just to make sure no one else was trying to come for that number one spot.

That afternoon after Cee left, I got a call from Maurice saying I could make a drop for him if I was still interested, so he could see how I felt about it. He was going to pay me four thousand for this drop, which was a far cry from forty thousand, but I wasn't about to turn it down. I didn't complain because it was a start and I knew I could work my hand later. I was determined to pay Cee back every dime and I meant it. I remembered I had stashed a lot of singles in a suitcase that I had left at the condo where Cee and I previously resided, so I made a mental note to go retrieve it after the run.

I had never counted the singles before because it was my just because money, but now I was desperate and needed every dollar I could scrounge up. I knew that after all those years of me and Cee throwing our singles in there daily, there had to be a good sum of cash in that suitcase. I called Cee and told him to tell Alicia that I would be coming over later so I could pick up some items I had left. Before ending our conversation, I made sure to tell him that I loved him; all he said in return was okay and hung up.

* * * *

I made the run for Maurice, which went well. All I had to do was pick a bag up and drop it off to the destination that he gave me. I didn't have to interact or talk to anybody. This was way too easy. He asked how much did I need to make, and being dead honest, I told him about fifty Gs. He said he didn't know if he had that much work for me, but could do twenty thousand if I could make two runs to Detroit before next week.

Without thinking, I happily agreed. I was to make the first run first thing in the morning and the next one that Saturday, and I was more than ready.

After arriving at our old place that night, I noticed Cee had moved his things back in. I also noticed that Alicia was acting really nasty and rude to me lately. Once she let me in I didn't say anything more than hi to her and kept it moving. I went about my business packing up some clothes and shoes that I never had a chance to come get after they seized the condo. The entire time I was in the closet packing up my things, Alicia stood in the doorway staring at me with a smug look on her face.

"Do you have a problem? I asked, breaking the silence.

"Do you?" she replied sarcastically.

"No, but you don't have to stand there and watch me. I got this."

"I don't trust your sneaky ass, and remember, you're in my house now."

"If you got something to say, just say it. I don't have a problem with you, so I don't know why you would have a problem with me Alicia."

I stood to my feet, now facing Alicia so she could get off whatever she had on her chest like a woman. Alicia had heart and I knew she wasn't going to let me size her up, so I stood there staring at her until she decided to talk.

"Yeah, I had a problem with you when you tried to play my brother," she finally said. "Yeah, I know everything. How that fag cheated on you in Atlanta and everything. You could have gave my brother something sleeping around like a nasty hoe. And you had the nerve to jack off his money after everything we've done for you?"

"How do you know my business, for one?" I asked, knowing I hadn't told Cee anything about what had happened in Atlanta except for the baby. "And for the record, you haven't done anything for me. I don't give a fuck about what you think you know or about what anybody has to say about me or what I do. This is between me and Cee, not me and you!"

"Not if I got anything to do with it, bitch. I know your business 'cause I made it my business when I started messing with J. He came crying on my shoulder, telling me how much he cared for you and all you did was shoot him down. He confided in me and told me everything about you, and all I did was suck it up like a sponge, stupid hoe," Alicia said, while twisting her scrawny neck from side to side with her hands on her hip, looking as ghetto as she truly was.

"Sorry baby girl, but I don't know anyone by the name of J, and sadly you don't know what the fuck you're talking about," I replied, embarrassed. I quickly gathered up my belongings and brushed by her, heading for the door.

I was not about to stand there and argue with her young ass. I had more important things to do early in the morning and I didn't need my head filled with this bullshit.

"Just make sure you leave him alone!" Alicia yelled, yapping at the lips, following behind me as I headed towards the door to leave. "I'm the reason why he hasn't been answering or returning your calls when you get lonely. Jarvis is with me now. How you like dem apples, hoe?" she concluded while giggling.

I stopped in my tracks. It felt as if she had just stabbed me in my back with an invisible knife and turned it to add insult to injury. Tears instantly welled up in my eyes as I began thinking about everything I had confided in with Jarvis. He was the one telling all my business, not Shelly. I knew he was weak, but damn, at the end of the day I thought he was one of my true friends. He was the only other person I considered my best friend other than Shelly. He basically knew everything about my entire life and had the audacity to run his mouth to this reckless bitch.

It all made sense now. It was never Shelly telling my business, but Alicia, and I now felt like a fool for ruining our friendship for nothing. I stood, paralyzed, fuming inside. I realized if Alicia had already told Cee everything that Jarvis could have told her, I knew it was over for me, for good.

I had to get home and get some rest before leaving for my run the next morning. I left the condo crushed and wounded without saying another word to Alicia. Even though Alicia may had ruined my relationship, I was still hell bent on paying Cee back, even if I had already totally lost his heart.

Chapter Twenty-Two

I got out of the bed around four that morning from just lying there because I couldn't sleep all night. All I could think about was the betrayal of Jarvis and how Alicia flipped out on me like that. Lord knows I wanted to beat her ass, but I knew I couldn't lay a hand on her if I had plans on staying in good graces with her brother. I hadn't talked to Cee since then, so I didn't know if Alicia had mentioned anything to him about our run-in or not. I planned on asking him to dinner and telling him everything myself so he didn't have to hear it from a third party.

I called Shelly, who I knew would be still asleep, so I could get her voicemail and apologize for wrongly accusing her of telling my business. I wasn't ready to talk to her because I had too much going on in my head and didn't have a chance to come up with a sincere enough apology to tell her. After leaving a brief message on her voicemail, I left my house to go meet Maurice so I could pick up the package.

When I got to Maurice's so-called home, he was acting really strange. I didn't know if it was because it was early in the morning or if he didn't want me to notice that he was there with another female, but

197

whatever he had going on was my last concern and I really I didn't care. I had more important things on my mind to worry about. After giving me the directions to the drop-off spot, he planted a quick peck on my lips, and basically pushed me out of his front door.

The drive to Detroit was approximately four hours. These trips were too easy. I planned on working something out with Maurice so I could make these runs more often. I stopped to get some gas in the rental car I was driving and to get some food because I was starving from not eating anything of substance in over two days. With all the other things that were going on in my head, I had forgotten to grab something to eat before I left the house. This trip allowed me the chance to clear my mind and think about what I was going to tell Cee and Shelly when I returned home.

In the car, I prayed aloud to God that Cee and Shelly would both forgive me because I was deeply sorry for everything I had previously done to ruin our relationship. I also prayed and asked God to forgive me for all my sins, and how I had accepted the fact that my baby was taken from me. Not knowing who my baby's father was would have been a total mess anyway. I wouldn't be caught on Maury with three different possibilities embarrassing the shit out of me. One, a hustler that I was still in love with; one, a bitch that couldn't keep his mouth shut; and lastly one, a bisexual to top it all off. I was ashamed as hell to even think that I had put myself in that kind of predicament.

I had to clear my mind and get myself together so I could focus on what I was doing. Finally at the destination, I slowly rode around the multi-level buildings searching for the address I had on the paper Maurice had given me. I slowed down and stopped at the building that matched the address where I was supposed to deliver the package. This time, I was to wait for the door to open and close before dropping the bag off at the door.

I waited there for about ten minutes, but still no sign of a door opening. I tried to call Maurice so he could call whomever and let them know I was here, but he didn't answer. Just as I began to dial Cee's number to invite him to dinner, I noticed familiar lights approaching from behind me.

I tried to slowly pull off like I was at the wrong place, but then three other police cars pulled up after the first one, blocking me in. An officer jumped out of his cruiser and yelled through his speaker for me to get out of the car with my hands up. All I could do was sit there in shock. I couldn't believe that this was actually happening to me. I was scared shitless and didn't want to make a wrong move, causing one of them to end up shooting me for no reason. I knew there were drugs involved within these runs, but I didn't know what kind or how much. Stupidly, I never looked in the bags that Maurice gave me. Instead, I just rolled with it because my eyes were only on the hefty cash prize in the end.

Knowing that this was a set up and that my life was officially over, I instantly started crying uncontrollably, kicking, punching, and screaming into the air like a crazy person. The officer demanded again that I exit the car with my hands up. After a brief moment I contained myself, dried my eyes, sucked in an enormous amount of oxygen, got out of the car, and threw my hands in the air. The officer tackled me to the ground like I was a stone-cold criminal and informed me that I was under arrest for the possession of narcotics with the intent to sell.

There was nothing left that I could say to defend myself, because I had been caught red-handed. I tightly closed my eyes as the officer placed the steel handcuffs tightly around my wrist and read me my Miranda rights. I silently prayed again that God heard all of my prayers, because I wouldn't be able to personally give Cee or Shelly my apologies they deserved after this.

Chapter Twenty-Three

After countless continuances and unnecessary waiting, Mr. Reed, my lawyer, informed me that I was facing five to ten years in prison if I didn't want to take the deal that they came up with, and had to wait for my next court date to get the final verdict. Thankfully, Cee paid Mr. Reed in advance so I wouldn't have to deal with a measly public defender. Shelly and my sister, Angie, showed up to court a couple of times, which confirmed that God had indeed delivered my prayers. Marie came whenever Cee showed up to my court dates and Jarvis even showed up once. I didn't blame him for what he had done because I had hurt him bad. I forgave him and decided to let the past be the past so I could move on with my life. I wasn't sure if everyone showed up just to be nosy or because they really cared, but it was nice to see familiar faces every time I went to court.

I thought Cee would have gotten me out on bail, which was only ten thousand dollars, but I was thankful that he cared enough to get me the lawyer. Mr. Reed informed me that after a couple of years served and with good behavior he would be able to try and get my time knocked down. He said my case looked good because I had no previous record besides the assault charges in Atlanta, which were later dropped. I didn't really care about serving the time because I felt like I was all alone and didn't have anyone that loved me or that I could love anymore. My life was officially over for three years at the least.

Sitting in jail was the last thing I could have predicted would happen to me after all my dedication and determination to make my life and relationship stable. I would have rather settled for a kid with five possibilities as fathers than to have to deal with a situation like this. Who would really want to mess with a girl that has done time in prison but another felon or guy that could relate to her and understand her situation. And, I knew I wouldn't be able to get a decent job with a drug trafficking stamp on my background report. My life was screwed.

I couldn't determine if going through this was all worth remaining kosher with Cee. Hell, I could have just manned up and let him know the money was gone and he would get it when I got it, but that wasn't me. I never wanted anyone to look at me like I was less than the naturally good person that I was. I didn't regret anything that I had done because I realized that life is full of unimaginable lessons to be learned, and there were still some areas in my life that needed improvement. Unfortunately, this time away was going to be my dose of harsh reality.

* * * *

Who would have ever thought that me, Desiree Wright, Miss Have It All and Miss Know It All, would trade in all my designer apparel for a tacky orange jumpsuit. As I sat in my cell the first night, all I could think of was that I was amazed that my loyalty ran so deep for niggas to the point that I opted to trade in my freedom to spare theirs. Cee was one thing, because that was my heart. But to protect the identity of a nigga who I had just met was another. I had so much hatred in my heart from the very thought of being locked up that I was going to personally be sure that Maurice paid the piper.

Lately, when I would look in the mirror, my reflection would often frighten me as I viewed the image staring back at me. The look on my face was starting to resemble that demonic look Cee often made when his heart turned cold. I was also turning into something cold, and I wasn't liking it.

I realized it was never the love of money that landed me in prison, but the love I had for Cee that caused me to think irrationally and let the streets once again get the best of me. I can honestly say that death is painful and hard to get over, but so is love. Forget until death do you part, because the pain from love can hurt just as bad as someone passing away, and I was feeling the wrath of it.

Jail was lonely but peaceful after the first few weeks. I was very standoffish when I first came in because these females were not like me and I didn't deserve to be shacked up with criminals. Most of the day, I would cry and refuse to eat, but after a few days, that got old.

Of course I was tested by females who said I thought I was too good or too cute to be locked up. They picked with me day in and out until I made it known I was no punk. After being provoked one time too many, I had to go toe to toe with some female. They then knew not to let the pretty face fool them. After the few fights I was involved in, I managed to stay to myself most of the time and didn't associate with too many people. These females had serious issues and loved to stay in everyone's business and cause drama. My charges and lifestyle was normal compared to theirs.

I met some cool, sane chicks who weren't about petty drama all the time. The main female that I bonded with instantly was a girl named Lanique. She was in here because she tried smuggling some coke into a prison when she was going to visit her fiancé and got busted. She was a couple of years younger than I was, but we related to each other very well, so we hung with each other most of the time.

I received letters and pictures of my handsome, little nephew every now and then from my sister. My mom even wrote once, criticizing me and my lifestyle. I instantly ripped up the letter and never wrote back. Every day, I would wait patiently for a letter to come from Cee or Shelly, but as the days passed I never received anything from either one. I had no idea if either of them had forgiven me for my stupidity, and I knew it didn't make matters any better that I was locked up.

I never tried calling anyone, because I didn't want to run up anybody's phone bill or be a nuisance. I knew personally how it was to constantly receive unwanted calls from lonely inmates, and I wasn't going to be the one. I thought about Cee constantly and beat myself up thinking about what I could have done differently to change the outcome of my situation. I wanted my old life back, but most of all, I wanted Cee.

I read a lot of books that Lanique let me borrow, which helped me escape from the life I was currently living and focus on the characters in the books and their issues. I typically read books that were similar to my situation: *A Gangster's Girl*, by Chunichi; *A Hustler's Wife*, by Nikki Turner; and *Let That Be the Reason*, by Vickie Stringer were just a few. These books let me know I was not alone in this game, and there would be plenty more females in the future that would endure similar adventures as I have.

One night, as my mind ran reckless, I sat thinking and visualizing what I could do to turn my situation around to be a positive role model, instead of representing and portraying a fabulous lifestyle with a hustler like I had intended when I first got with Cee. This time, I wanted to help girls not to end up like me. Being in here, I'd learned that there were several girls like myself that grew up with no home training on how to be a strong woman, how to be content without a man, or how to even love themselves. Most girls were in here because of some crime dealing with a man. If they had the proper teaching or training beforehand, they would know how to make wiser choices to break the cycle.

I wrote down several ideas to start up a home or center for underprivileged girls where they could learn the importance of education, money management, home-making skills, and self-love. I also wanted to become more involved in church. I knew it had to be because of God's grace that I had managed to survive all the situations that I had been through in my life. If nothing else, I would make it my number one priority to read the Bible every night while behind bars.

The next day after I finished beating Lanique in a card game, once again, the other inmates scurried and gathered around the security desk as the C.O. called out names for mail. Mail call every day for these women was like Christmas. They would anxiously wait to see if letters or pictures would come from their family, children, or significant others. Lanique and I both knew we weren't receiving anything because her fiancé was in the hole for a week and I had just received my monthly package from my sister last week.

Lanique began dealing the next hand of cards, when shockingly I heard my name being called for mail. I remained seated and yelled to Rose, the oldest and wisest inmate in our area, to bring my mail over to me.

She strutted over to my table, my mail in hand, while grinning from ear to ear with her wide, toothless smile. "Looks like somebody's got a love letter," she said, swinging my letter from side to side.

I snatched the letter from her and blankly stared at the white envelope, wondering who it could be from.

"Get out of here, gummy, and put your dentures in, will ya'?" Lanique joked, while waving Rose away.

Rose skipped off and went back over to the security desk to be nosy and to offer inspiration to the women whose prayers to receive mail remained unanswered.

"I'll be back to whoop yo' ass in a minute," I said to Lanique, as I got up and began walking up to my cell.

I was shocked to have received an unfamiliar envelope, which didn't have a return address on it, and prayed it was from Cee or Shelly. After entering my cell, I sat on the edge of my bunk bed and carefully tore open the envelope. I tried to contain my emotions and tears as I scanned the familiar scribble-scrabble on the paper and smiled from ear to ear. I wiped away the tears that escaped my eyes and covered my mouth so no one could hear me sobbing as I read the letter silently to myself.

July 5th

Hey, Desi. Sorry I hadn't written you earlier. It's been busy out here in these streets so you know I'm on my grind. I got my money right now, so I'm going to put some money on your books to help you out a little. Your lawyer said he should be able to get your time cut down after a couple years, so don't go getting into no trouble with your fly-ass mouth. I miss you, girl, and I think about you all the time. I couldn't let you just sit in there and rot because you always looked out for me no matter what we went through.

I'd rather you had left me alone and developed yourself as a woman instead of trying to get me back after you found out about Darius. Women don't realize that once a man is scorned it's worse than any woman's pain, because we will never truly forgive or forget what has been done to us. We will bring up that shit at the drop of a dime and won't release it from our hearts no matter how hard you try to repair the damage. I love you and it will take some time for me to heal and totally forgive you for what you have done. I promise to work on not holding anything against you, especially since you are in this predicament mainly because of me.

My sister told me things about you that I didn't know anything about. I found it difficult deciding if I even wanted to believe it or not. She said she's in a relationship with some guy that you were messing around with and that y'all weren't cool anymore. I know how Alicia can get, and I didn't know if she was saying all of that out of anger or what, so I just let it go. I registered for some classes at Cincinnati State for business like you always suggested, but I haven't started yet. I'm going to make my money work for me instead of me constantly working for my money out here in these streets. I talked to Shelly and she told me what really happened between y'all. I don't know if you heard, but she lives with Will now, crazy huh? They make me so sick sometimes, but they cool. I look at them the same way they probably looked at us back in the day, but I'm glad they're happy together.

I wanted to apologize for the things I did to you in the past, and I also have a confession to make. The day I gave you that ring I wanted to ask you to marry me. I wanted to straighten things out with Terra first before taking that next step with you. I was scared to make that kind of commitment with you at the time, so that's why I made a promise to you instead. My mom told me that you gave her the ring before you got locked up, which made me upset because I told you to never take it off and I was dead serious. When you get out, I want you to have it back because you are and will always be my first love.

I know I should have never played with your heart, because I now realize a woman's heart is the path to her soul. I feel I messed that up for you, and it's my fault that you are in there now.

It's late and I am tired as hell after the party we had tonight, but I felt the need to write you before I went to sleep. I don't know when I will be able to write again and I don't want you to be waiting around or anticipating another letter. So, let's just say this will be my last letter, and if you get another, it will be a gift from me.

I don't think I can ever say it enough, but I love you, Desiree, and please try to keep your head up. Forever and always my soldier girl.

P.S. We had a party tonight and I couldn't stop thinking how much I would have loved to have you here by my side. I was so ecstatic after I received my paternity papers in the mail this morning because it proved that Darius was never mine, so the crew got together tonight to celebrate. I love you again, kid, and when you get out, I will be waiting for you with open arms just like you were there for me.

Your Love Always,
Cee

Made in the USA
Columbia, SC
19 August 2019